Donald

Donald's parents have great difficulty having children, so when Donald is born, they feel doubly blessed that their son is such a beautiful baby. To Donald, this blessing soon becomes a curse as his beauty does not fade as he ages, and he is constantly mistaken for a female. Tired of these mistakes as he enters adulthood, he is doubly frustrated as he is also mistaken for a homosexual. Hoping to lose himself in a larger city, Donald foregoes college and moves to Atlanta. A new friend, Rita, convinces Donald that he can escape the assumption that he is a woman or gay by masquerading as a woman in the dazzling Atlanta nightlife. Soon, Donald parlays his singing talent into a career as "DeeDee."

Author
Terry Collins

For information, contact Terry Collins at
collinsterry@live.com

Published and distributed: Terry Collins

ISBN: 978-1-61658-776-5

First printing Instant Publishing Co. January 2010

Senior Editor: Keith "Doc" Suggs

Co-editors: Jackie Yelvington, Marjorie Key, Verneice Collins and Jessica Collins

Typist: Jamberlyne Voss

Cover designed by Jackie Yelvington and Terry Collins

Printed in the U.S.A.

This novel is dedicated to Keith "Doc" Suggs and to my "Boo," Jackie "Y."

With Much Love...

acknowledgments

Thank you, Lord, for this opportunity; through God, all things are possible. To my mother, Vera Harper, affectionately known as "O.G.", thanks so much for always believing in me. To Keith "Doc" Suggs, who is my friend, confidant, and a very talented writer, thank you ever so much; this novel would not have come to fruition had it not been for your great vision, time , energy, and expertise; I can't thank you enough for everything you did and are continuing to do. To Evangelist Cassie Young Hare, author of ***The Hole in My Heart***, and my new found friend; thanks for sharing so much important information with me and your willingness to give so much of your time;

you helped me tremendously. To Linda Faye Reddick, thanks for telling Evangelist Hare about me and making it possible for us to meet. I will always believe that God had a hand in that also. Minus Adams, my very best friend; thank you for the support you have shown throughout the years and most of all, for being a good listener; after our many conversations, I would feel energized, motivated and encouraged. To my typist, Jamberlyne L. Voss, thanks for coming on board and helping to put it all together.

To my children thanks for **supporting** me and always believing in my love for you.

Brenda, my sister, thanks for your constant support. Marjorie Key, thanks for reading my manuscript and sharing your kind and uplifting comments. Last but not least, I want to thank my "Boo," Jackie "Y." I will never be able to thank you enough for all of your help, support, encouragement, and ***just having my back***. And to those of you who purchase my book, I sincerely thank you, too. Read and enjoy ***Donald***.

Terry Collins

1

"The Chattanooga Skyline"

Nothing says home to me like the Chattanooga skyline. Stand here with me and look across the mountains and the other landmarks - the famous, the infamous, and the gauche. If you have ever driven through the Old South, you cannot have missed the roofs; those painted barns that read “See Rock City” without wondering: “What the hell is Rock City?” And Rock City is a microcosm of greater Chattanooga, an inspiration at every turn to ask: “What the hell?”

My name is Donald. Pleased to meet you. I am probably unlike anyone you know. Oh, you may think you know someone like me, or that people like me exist, but you don’t really know me, because what you assume is not anywhere near the truth. I’ve written about my life so that you will understand that you don’t know me because once you open your mind and allow yourself to truthfully know me, you will experience the municipal question: “What the hell?" And that's okay. I often look in the mirror and ask the same question. I'm taking you with me on a journey of self-discovery and maybe together we'll come up with the answer that I have yet to ascertain.

Like I was saying, the Chattanooga skyline is home. And once you begin to study the city more closely, you will find the campus of the University of Tennessee at Chattanooga. The students call themselves "the Mocs." Don't go there. We aren't talking about now; we're talking about autumn, 1981. Because to know me, first, you need to know my parents.

If you look carefully, you'll see a 1969 Chevrolet Impala parking in front of the women's dormitory. That's my father,

Bill Danforth. He hops out of the car. He has a deep tan complexion and is dressed in slacks, a shirt, and a light pullover sweater." He is almost to the door of the dorm when Betty Hanson, his girlfriend, who will become my mother, comes out of the dorm. She, too, is upper middle class black and is prep-school dressed. She runs to him, hugs him, and kisses him on the cheek. They return to his car. He holds the door for her, and then walks around to get in on his side. She scoots to the middle of the seat. They both buckle their seat belts. I mention that to indicate to you that my parents always do what is expected of them. They would never think to belittle or to be impolite or to run a stop sign. Poet Don L. Lee once observed that some Negroes were so cool that they would even stop for green lights. My father wouldn't go that far, but you get the picture.

Bill starts the car, shifts into drive, and the car moves forward. See? Just as expected. Two black virgins out on their weekly date. "Oh, Bill, I wish we were already married," purrs my Mom. "I'm sick of living in that dorm."

My Dad grimaces a little. "Now, Betty, we agreed to wait until next spring right after graduation. Besides, if you're not in the dorm, how will you ever be able to find bridesmaids?"

Mom giggles. "Silly. Maybe I should move into the sorority house."

Dad studies Mom closely, but not

enough to take his eyes off the road. “I thought you liked the dorm.”

My Mom’s shoulders rise in one of her now famous shrugs. “Well, I do, but there are some new girls there this term. I’m not; well, completely comfortable with them.”

Dad presses her. “Why not?”

“They say things.”

“What kinds of things?”

“Bill.” Mom hesitates. “Do you think we’re,” she wrinkles her nose, “black enough?”

“What?”

“These new girls." They think that I’m - they tell me that I’m white except for my complexion.

“That's nonsense.”

“Is it? We both dress like white students. We speak like white people. We have, you know, middle class ambitions.”

“Betty, do you feel guilty about being black?”

“No, of course not. I’m proud to be black.”

“So am I. Do you think I’m any less black because I wear Brooks Brothers instead of a dashiki?”

The car pulls into the Shoney's parking lot. The "Big Boy" smiles down on them like a benign god. Betty looks at the cherub, but he offers her no answer. She responds with her own. “No.”

“Because if you do? Well, just turn

the clock back twenty years and see if these clothes make any difference had you and I wanted to eat here at Shoney's."

"We couldn't. We couldn't have used their rest room. We couldn't even drink their water."

"I'm proud of what my parents did in the struggle. So proud that I'm doing what they want. They want me to go to college." Dad parks the car making certain that he is perfectly within the lines. "They want me to get a business degree and keep wealth in the community. And they want me to be an American."

Mom places a nurturing hand on the back of Dad's neck. "Our parents are so much alike. That's why mine want me to teach. They want me to serve as an example to show black and white kids what's possible in America."

"As soon as I graduate, I'll step into a good job. And after just a year, I'll open my own insurance agency. I want that nice house in the suburbs with two cars in the garage." Dad looks into Mom's eyes and smiles, lovingly. "A beautiful wife - "

Mom utters a rare interruption. "Thank you very much."

Dad acknowledges her with a big smile. "- and two kids."

"Just two?"

Dad grins that famous grin of his, the one that can sell insurance to anyone. "All right," as many kids as you can stand.

They'll all go to college and be successful and get married and have kids and be happy." Dad gets out of the car. He walks around to let Mom out, and as the gentleman he always is he opens the door for her, offers his hand which Mom takes, and she gets out. "And they'll be just as proud to be black."

"And I'm very proud of you."

It is the rarest of occasions when my mother

or my father display public displays of affection. But this is one of those times and they share a quick, chaste kiss. After the kiss, Dad gestures to the restaurant. "And we'll bring them all to Shoney's to eat Big

Boys."

Mom puts her arm on his and says, "And strawberry pie."

2

“Insurance”

Once Mom and Dad were married, Mom began teaching and Dad took all that business training and opened an insurance agency. To my people, insurance is an interesting concept: Some choose no insurance at all, preferring to gamble on everything. A small few choose not to gamble and to insure everything.

The most popular of all policies is burial insurance. Having an impressive funeral may not guarantee entry into heaven, but it will electrify those who come to the funeral armed with fans and decked out in impressive hats. My dad did very well in the insurance business and became a pillar of the black community of Chattanooga. Nobody seemed to mind, much, that he sounded white when he talked.

Dad went from a storefront to a building all his own, and Dad was elected president of the black businessmen's association. He and Mom built a large suburban home in Chattanooga's only upscale neighborhood for blacks. So they decided that they were ready to have a child.

" . . . and so far as we can tell, the fallopian tubes are entirely closed, as if the tubes are not even there," said the gynecologist.

My dad simply couldn't accept the fact that all this work was not going to be for the outcome he expected. "That just can't be."

"I urge you to get a second opinion," advised the doctor, "but speaking bluntly, I don't know of any surgical procedure that would alter the condition."

Mom was in shock. "So I can never bear children."

The doctor shook his head. "Not necessarily. We are making great strides in what the laymen call 'test-tube babies.' I seriously doubt that we could harvest your own eggs but - "

Mom interrupted him. "You make me sound like a chicken farm."

The doctor stiffened, realizing he was

speaking to two relatively sophisticated individuals. "I'm sorry. I seriously doubt that you could be the biological mother, but a donor could give us ova which we could fertilize with Mr. Danforth's sperm. There is nothing wrong with your womb itself. We could implant a fertilized egg, and you could carry it to full term."

Hesitantly, my dad asked the doctor.

"Are there no other options?"

Deferring to my mother, the doctor replied. "Mr. Danforth could also impregnate a surrogate mother - through artificial insemination, of course."

My mom continued to prod him. "What else?"

The doctor shrugged. "Well, of course, you could adopt," he answered. "There is never a shortage of black babies."

Dad had bought a "brand new" 1984 Cadillac to celebrate a bonus he had received from a national burial insurance firm. The new car did not make the trip back from the doctor's office any more comfortable.

Tears formed in my mother's eyes.

"Bill, right now, I'm not comfortable with any of those so-called options."

"Me, neither the whole thing is such a shock."

"Bill, I am so sorry."

"Betty, it's not your fault. It's not anybody's fault."

"But I know how much you want children of our very own."

"That's true, but I wouldn't pick any 'fertile Myrtle' in the world as an alternative to you. It's you that I chose to spend the rest of my life with. I don't need kids, but I do need you."

My mom laughed. "Well."

Dad did not expect her laughter. "What?"

Through her tears, my mother smiled - as a bright sun beaming through the rain clouds. “I was just thinking about how glad I am to be a teacher.”

“Yeah?”

“Yeah, I may never have my own child, but each day, I get to have 180 that belong to someone else.”

Their stress was relieved by a barrage of laughter.

Bill reassured my mom. “We'll give it a rest, and then we'll make some sort of decision. There's no hurry.”

“I sure hope you don't mean give sex a rest.”

“Of course not!”

“Because I have the rest of the day off

and so do you."

"Right."

Snuggling closer to my dad, mom said, "Don't you think it would be a shame to waste it?"

"A crying shame."

"So let's go home and open a bottle of wine, put on that Donnie Hathaway album"

"Minnie Ripperton."

"All right, Minnie Ripperton, and enjoy the rest of the afternoon. The day won't be a total waste."

"No day with you is a total waste.

Unlike most kids, I've never felt uncomfortable about picturing my parents making love. I even hear the soundtrack of their love. Minnie Ripperton singing

"Loving You" and Donnie Hathaway singing “I’ll Love You More Than You’ll Ever Know.” There was always great music playing in our home - more about that later.

After dinner one night, they looked over papers and pamphlets on adoption. Mom was interested but distracted, nauseous, green. Dad was not paying attention. “Of course, we could get a child from overseas. China, maybe. Or - “
But Mom’s upset stomach kept her from pursuing adoption so they dropped the subject that night and didn’t pick it up again. Instead . . .

Bill and Betty went about their lives for five years watching other couples with their children playing in the park, Betty seeing the kids being dropped off by their parents at school, Bill seeing fathers and sons together dropping by his office to pay for insurance, seeing children seated on Santa's lap while Christmas shopping. Their sex lives were fine, of course; they loved each other. But it grew routine, and Dad was bothered by the fact that Mom seemed unsatisfied. “Is it me?”

“No, Bill. You're sensitive, caring, generous, and considerate”

“Then, what?”

“It's just that sometimes, I think that making love, as wonderful as it is, was meant to make babies. And we'll never have one.”

“I think it's time to look into

adoption."

"Let's not talk about it tonight, Bill."

"But we never talk about it and -"

"I agree. Adoption is our best option, and I
want to do it. Really, I just don't feel very well tonight. Something I ate, I guess."

"Just let me know when you're ready to discuss it."

"I will."

Betty was teaching a fourth grade geography class in 1984. "This red country right here is called Austria."

One of her students raised his hand. "I thought Austria was down off south of Asia."

Another student added, "Yeah, with

all those cute little koala bears and stuff."

Mom laughed. "That's Australia. They sound a lot alike. But they are completely different countries."

Another student raised his hand. "That's confusing."

But Mom was always good at explaining confusing things. "There's a Georgia just a few miles from here, but there's also a Georgia in the Soviet Union. There's a Paris, Tennessee and a Paris, France."

One of Mom's fourth graders whined. "How do we remember all that?"

"Well, as far as Eastern Europe and Asia Minor is concerned, you can remember this group of countries by remembering this little phrase: 'Austria got Hungary and fried Turkey in Greece." The kids laughed; Mom always thought laughter helped children remember everything. "Repeat it."

They did. And then, Mom collapsed.

3

"A Bump on the Head"

My mother is a survivor, a quality she passed on to me. When I was a child, I thought she was the most beautiful woman on the planet. Teaching small children exposed her to every disease known to man and a number of “accidents” the worst of which resulted in cracked ribs. Mom learned quickly to be on the lookout for unexpected puddles of urine.

While I doubted bruised ribs were a picnic, I think my resolve to teach the younger children of the village would have been shaken by the number of times that a child had walked up to her and vomited on her. Mom kept extra outfits at school after having to drive to and from home and change. It annoyed her that the car smelled like vomit.

This time was different. Picture my mom in a hospital bed with Dad seated on the bed beside her. There is a bump on her head. While waiting on the same doctor that my parents had seen about infertility, Mom asked, “What else could be wrong?”

Dad lifted his hands in his favorite “I don’t know” gesture, “We'll find out. The doctor said that it didn't have to be anything serious.”

The door opened. The doctor entered. “Mr. and Mrs. Danforth

Mom wouldn’t let him express the usual pleasantries. “What's wrong?”

The doctor smiled. “Surprisingly nothing.”

My father, whose insurance business had made him aware of all sorts of ailments that, could cause one to fall and bump one’s head, asked: “Nothing?”

With a sheepish grin, the doctor

repeated: “Nothing, and Betty is pregnant.”

Mother was shocked: “Pregnant?”

Dad examined the doctor with a piercing gaze: “You said -”

“I know what I said,” interrupted the doctor. “And even though I asked you to get a second opinion, I was correct in my assessment.”

Dad started to smile through his consternation. “Then, how -”

“Remember, I said that no surgery could correct the problem, but sometimes ‘Mother Nature’ comes along and fixes things. You remember ‘Mother Nature, ‘don‘t you? That commercial about margarine, ‘It's not nice to fool Mother Nature?” My mother nodded. “Well, this time Mother Nature has made a fool out of me. She fixed what medical science could not. And the good news is that you are going to have a baby!”

My father was still smiling yet seemed irritated. “Will it be all right?”

The doctor shrugged. “I'm not a psychic, Mr. Danforth. But there's no indication that the pregnancy's atopic. We'll watch Mrs. Danforth with extra care, but I'm willing to bet that everything will be perfectly normal. We'll be doing some more tests, but these are routine. Will you want to know the gender of the child?”

Mom was quick to answer. “No, I want it to be a

surprise."

Dad looked into her eyes, finally breaking into a broad smile and relaxing. "It's already a surprise. The most beautiful surprise in the world."

The doctor raised the clipboard in his hands. "I'll make a note," he said and did. "Arnneosyntesis. Do not reveal the gender of the fetus." Then, he put the clipboard to his side. "Amazing what we can know these days. Someday, we may even be able to custom design things like hair and eye color!"

As if staring down Dr. Mengele, Mom said, "That sounds horrible!"

Dad dismissed the doctor. "We'll be happy with our baby - "and hugged my mother "- no matter what."

Dad and Mom did all the things the doctors and the baby books told them to do back then, took all the vitamins, did all the exercises, and attended Lamaze classes. Dad was a great coach.

Mom continued to teach. The doctors gave them excellent reports. It was a super normal pregnancy. And one day while Mom was grading papers behind her desk, her water broke. Mom was "in the zone" as she often was when she was in deep concentration and she didn't notice, but as if in cosmic payback, a child turning in a paper slipped in the fluid. Mom was zipped to the hospital; Dad met her there and coached her through it, and I was born.

"It's a boy!"

My dad could not mask his delight that his child was a boy. Oh, he told everyone that he didn't care so long as the baby was healthy, but I came into the world male and loud. "My, what strong lungs!" observed the doctor handing me to a nurse. "He's going to be a singer!" he laughed, examining the placenta. "We have some more work to do here," he said, turning to my mom. "Would you like to hold your son?

"Please."

"What's his name?"

A nurse handed me first to my dad; he immediately handed me to Mom telling the doctor "We decided on Donald."

Cuddling me, my mom added, “We liked the sound of Donald Danforth.”

“Distinguished,” observed a nurse.

“Double D initials will make an impressive monogram,” said the doctor. “Nurse Wilson, massage the fundus, please; I've got a little bleeding here.” The nurse complied.

My father added, “We decided against William, Jr. We didn't want the ‘Big Bill, Little Bill’ business. And you’re right, Donald is a distinguished name. It means ‘He rules the world -

“Doctor, the flow seems to be increasing.” The nurse was concerned.

“Let me see.” The doctor took a look. “Oh, my.” Controlling his panic, he said,

"Bill, this probably isn't anything serious, but we need to stop Betty's bleeding here. So you need to step out of the room please."

"But - "

"Donald will join you in your room very soon." And in an attempt at humor, the doctor added, **"He be hongry!"**

My dad kissed my mom and left as ordered. As the team started to work on Mom, Dad saw the doctor turn aside to the nurse and say, "I'm going to need an anesthetist."

Mom made it through the surgery all right. She was in recovery nursing me when Dad showed up, loaded down with athletic equipment: a baseball glove, a basketball, a football, etc. and a dozen roses for Mom.

She asked him: "Are you planning on starting some teams or changing careers?"

"No, these are for Donald."

Mom laughed: "Donald can't come out and play right now; he's eating."

Dad put down the equipment and sat. "Wow. He's really hungry. Does it hurt?"

With a sly glance, Mom answered: "No more than you."

When the doctor returned, he asked: "And how are the Danforths?"

"All three of us are just fine?"

The doctor frowned a bit. "Well, not exactly."

Mom asked: "Donald's all right, isn't he?"

"Donald's perfect. But there was a

slight complication in the delivery - some tearing."

"But I'm all right?"

"We were able to repair the damage, and there should be no problems for you, but, I'm sorry, there is no chance that you will conceive another child."

"You said that before and - well, here's Donald."

"This time there is no chance whatsoever. Unless you change your mind and adopt, Donald will be an only child." The doctor exhaled. "But he certainly is a fine specimen."

Mom was still smiling. "Thank you, Doctor."

As the tired doctor leaned against the

wall, he said: “You know, I’m not supposed to show partiality, but I deliver babies all the time, and I must say that Donald is the finest baby that I've ever had the privilege to deliver.”

Dad was amused by this. “He is handsome, isn't he?”

“All those of us who deliver babies look for that one. Male or female? Black or white? This is my one. He wins the prize for most likely to succeed. The super-kid!”

My mother beamed. “Thank you, He is, isn't he?”

Dad grinned. “Yes, he is.”

4

“It’s a Boy!”

I’ve seen pictures of my parents decorating the nursery. Everything was very masculine, very blue. In the front yard, they had placed a wooden stork holding up a sign that says: “It’s a boy." My parents had bought a blue stroller. They dressed me in a

Tennessee orange football uniform and wrapped me in a blue blanket and took me down the sidewalk, very proud. And it was on that sidewalk that they met an elderly couple, Annie and Maxie,
who were walking a few blocks from our home. Their observations were not necessarily prophetic, but they did make points that spoke to the way that Americans see the roles of gender. They studied me carefully as my parents stopped, beaming proudly.

"Oh, my, how adorable," Annie said.

Her husband pointed at my tiny orange uniform. "And a Tennessee Volunteer!"

My mother knew the answer to the question even before she asked: “Would you like to hold the baby?”

Annie looked as if she’d been truly blessed. “Oh, could I, please?”

“Sure,” my dad said picking me up and placing me in Annie’s arms.

Annie cooed at me. “You are such a pretty little thing!”

And Maxie became the first of many to ask the question: “What's her name?”

My mother explained: “His name is Donald.”

Dad saw that he needed to be more emphatic while trying not to offend the elderly couple. “He's a boy.”

Annie couldn’t believe her ears.

"You're joking."

My dad couldn't understand why these people didn't grasp that I was male. "No," he smiled. "No joke. He's simply a good looking boy."

Still amazed, Maxie said, "It's just that boys are never this pretty."

Mom saw no problem with this. "Well, this one is."

Maxie made a noise that startled me. "Harumph!"

Annie tried to calm me. "Well, Donald, you can be the most beautiful baby and be a man, can't you?"

Maxie turned to my dad. "Our girls were pretty, but our boys looked like little bulldogs."

Annie confided in my parents. “We had eight.”

And Mom had so much trouble having one? “Eight?”

Maxie nodded. “Four of each. Four pretty girls, and four ugly bulldogs.”

Annie smiled slyly. “Well, the boys all look like you.” And then she placed me in Maxie’s hands.

Maxie looked into my eyes. “You gonna play football, Donnie?” He growled; I sensed danger and started to cry.

Annie nudged her husband. “You old bear! You're scaring him!”

My dad took me back from Maxie and put me back in the stroller. Bill tried not to look irritated, but he was never able to deal with his feelings where I was concerned, not when someone else caused me any distress.

Annie excused Maxie's behavior. "Good-bye, Donald. Don't let this senile old man bother you. He's just jealous because he's not as good looking as you are!"

Mom smiled politely. "We'd better be getting along."

Bill began to push the stroller away. "Good-bye."

Annie responded, "Good-bye. Good-bye Donald," as she and Maxie walked the other way. "I swear, Maxie, you scared that little baby on purpose."

Maxie grunted again. "Harumph! The boy's too pretty to be a football player. Bet he's gonna be one of them male cheerleaders."

Annie looked at him with a hard gaze. "Maxie! They'll hear you!"

"I didn't say he was a 'sweet boy,' Annie May."

"You said he was going to be a cheerleader."

"That don't mean he gotta be a 'sweet boy.' I always wanted to be a male cheerleader. They get to handle all the girl cheerleaders!" And Maxie handled Annie. She pretended that she didn't like it, but she giggled just the same.

My parents encouraged me to talk at an early age. They would also spell out words with alphabet blocks. Mom would tell me everything about what she was doing, carefully pronouncing every word precisely. I would smile and play, but I was quiet.

Dad worried. “Do you think he'll ever talk?”

Mom had bought some new draperies; she was preparing them to hang on curtain rods. “Of course, honey. He's perfectly fine. He'll be explaining insurance policies and detailing complex offensive plays to a football team in no time at all!”

My parents laughed. My dad arranged my alphabet blocks in formation for an offensive play. “I guess. Do you need some help with those curtains?”

And I looked up from the blocks and said: “Draperies.”

There was a moment of silence while my parents were amazed. Then, Mom broke the silence. “Isn't that sweet? His first word!”

My dad was vexed. "Draperies"? Mom picked me up and kissed me. “Bill, he's talking!”

I repeated with enthusiasm: “Draperies!”

“But ‘Draperies‘? I was expecting ‘Mama’ or ‘Dada.’ Not ‘draperies.’”

“Donald was with me when the man at the store was explaining the difference between curtains and draperies. I guess Donald just picked it up. You know kids.”

“I don't know kids.” My father shook his head. “I could tell you the subtle differences in insurance policies, but I don’t know the difference between curtains and draperies.”

“Curtains are more like a screen.” My mom gestured at what she was hanging. “Draperies are hung more loosely. These are draperies.”

And I echoed, “draperies!” I laughed and clapped my hands.

My mother was so pleased with me. “That's Mama's good boy. See Bill, he's talking.” Dad smiled but was not quite sure.

Another month and I had pulled myself up on some furniture and was standing. I moved about, but I wouldn't let go of the furniture. Dad was reading the business section of the paper. He looked at me and said, “Donald? Walk over to Daddy. Come on,” and put out his hands. “Walk to Daddy.” I turned and carefully stepped toward my father. I giggled as I came into his arms, so excited to get there. I looked into the radiance that was my father’s face. Dad took me back to the same place and then returned to his chair, calling to my mother. “Show Mama, Donald. Walk to Daddy.”

This time, I walked with more confidence. Dad proudly hoisted me in the air. Mom smiled up into my face. “Good boy! Isn't that wonderful, Bill? He's walking!” Dad grinned and placed me back at my original starting point. “ I know.”

Watch him walk. Walk to Daddy, Donald, Donald walks again.” I walked, but not in a straight line. “It's probably just my imagination, but did you see him? Just like a running back dodging tacklers!” Mom didn’t see it that way. “When he walked to me just then. Kind of a spinning step like following a blocker through - “

“Bill, are you nuts? He's a baby, for Christ's sake!” She took me from him and hugged me. “Every part of his body is trying to maintain balance.” She encouraged me. Good boy!”

“You're right, Betty. I don't know what I was thinking. I don't have any experience with this father thing. I want him to - “

Mom looked both amused and sarcastic. “What did you want him to do? Run by you with that football you bought him and stiff-arm you?”

Dad looked a little guilty. “Well, no.”

5

“The Twos Were not so Terrible”

I was a healthy baby who learned how to talk and walk very quickly. My parents told me that everything was fun to me, everything interesting. I’d been given photographs of my mom taking great joy in my growth and development but not many photos of my dad. Mom explained that Dad was always holding the camera.

I was always willing to please, including potty training. I understood the concept very quickly. In an attempt to enable the masculine perspective, my father stacked some encyclopedias by the toilet and placed me upon them. "Okay, son. Do like Daddy? Pee-pee in the potty." I laughed, stepped down from the encyclopedias, and sat on my potty chair. I didn't notice, but this perplexed my father.

Music was always a part of the home I grew up in. Mom and Dad had their favorites, and any activity around our house was orchestrated. The music of their generation was recorded on vinyl and the large format of the record covers provided canvases for a glorious cultural tapestry.

I remember sitting on the floor of the living room with my dad. He had spread the album covers around us. The bright colors and smiling faces of those enthralled by creating music made me smile. Dad shared his enthusiasm: "Okay, Donald. Nothing is more important to a black man than his education in soul music. Now, this is Aretha Franklin." He held up the album that included Aretha's cover of Otis Redding's "Respect."

After allowing me to study Aretha's cherubic face for a while, Dad put it aside and chose another. "And this is Ray

Charles." Ray beamed from the cover of Love Country Style. I smiled back.

"So who do you want to listen to?"

I thought carefully. Then, light dawned in my eyes, and I responded with eagerness: "Barbra!"

"What?"

I stood up and walked over to the record library. I pulled out the soundtrack from Funny Girl and brought it back to my father. "Barbara."

Mom had been in the kitchen. Wonderful smells wafted in when she opened the door. "What are my men doing?"

Dad, studying the cover of Funny Girl responded: "Music Appreciation 101."

Mom sat down with us. “Good. What artists are we studying?”

“Well, our class was on Aretha and Ray,” he said. “I'm trying to get Donald to choose, and I think he wants Barbra.”

“Oh?” Mom took the soundtrack from Dad and took the shiny vinyl disk out, placing it on the turntable. “Okay.”

Dad asked, “What are you doing?”

Mom set the controls on the amplifier. “Playing my Funny Girl album. Donald just loves it.”

"Don't Rain on My Parade" started. Hearing it, I shouted: “Barbra!”

Dad looked quizzically into Mom’s eyes. “My son likes Barbra Streisand?”

Mom smiled: “Your son loves Barbra

Streisand."

Almost catatonic, Dad said, "No."

After a period to regain his concentration, Dad turned the music off. He sat down in front of me again. "Donald, soul music is the music of our people. R & B! Now, choose. Aretha or Ray?"

I smiled, not understanding: "Barbra!"

Dad shook his head. "No, Donald, Barbra's not here. Aretha or Ray."

I asked, "Barbra?"

"No. Aretha or Ray!"

I smiled, changing my mind. "Judy." Dad looked at Mom for an explanation. "Judy?"

Mom explained. "He also loves Judy Garland. You know my album? Judy in Concert at the London Palladium?

This frustrated my father. “How about the Village People?”

I jumps up and formed the letters. “Y.M.C.A.!!!”

Dad slapped his own face. “Oh, no.”

Mom tried to reason with him. “It’s just music.” And added, that’s your album, remember.”

Dad protested. “It was a gift.”

Betty took Dad’s shoulders in her hands. “We used to play it and laugh.”

Frustrated again, Dad began, “I just want him to - “

But Mom tried to stop him. “Music Appreciation 101 is over for today.”

“No, it's not.” Dad explained slowly. “Donald, listen to these two and tell me which one to play. This is Ray."

Bill played. "Hit the Road Jack" by Ray Charles.

I stood up and danced to the music. After a verse or two, Bill changed the record to "Think" by Aretha Franklin and played it up through the first chorus. I also danced to this one.

"And that was Aretha," Dad said. "Now, Donald, which one would you like Daddy to play?"

I smiled coyly. "Bette Midler!"

Dad threw up his hands. "No, son. Ray or Aretha?"

I had finally understood the limitation of my choices, so I began to chant. "'Retha! 'Retha! 'Retha! 'Retha! . . ."

Dad smiled satisfied and let Aretha's album play.

Christmas was always special in our home, too. I do remember having my picture made with Santa but I don't remember having questions about whether Santa Claus was black or white. I also remember the department store line with Mom working on my hair while Dad coached me. "Now, remember, Donald, tell Santa that you want Legos and a truck and a baseball bat.

I was always good at remembering series of words. "Legos and a truck and a baseball bat."

Dad smiled at my mother. "He's got it."

Repetition helped. “Legos and a truck and a baseball bat” said over and over as we got closer to Santa.

Santa seemed more concerned with the photo than the Legos. Maybe that‘s how he got paid. He told me to “Look at the camera.” I did and the "elf” took our picture.

When the elf nodded, Santa asked, “Now, what would you like Santa to bring you for Christmas?”

I recalled, “Legos and a truck and a baseball bat.”

Apparently Santa’s memory worked the same way. “Legos and a truck and a baseball bat?”

I looked up into his eyes. “Can I

whisper?"

Santa smiled. "Of course you can."

So I whispered in Santa's ear. Santa looked into my eyes, thoughtfully, and nodded. I hugged Santa and gave Santa a kiss on the cheek. Then, I climbed down from Santa's lap and went over to my mother. My dad walks over to Santa and tipped him. Dad was always a generous tipper. "Santa, what did my son whisper to you?"

"That's confidential, sir. You know, like a priest or a psychiatrist?"

Dad didn't buy the association. "Is it something for him that wasn't on his list?" Santa was hesitant to answer.

"What then? How can I get it for him if I

don't know what it is?"

Santa shook his head. "Your son said that - I only can get this for - "

Bill pressed him. "Keep it real, Santa. Be indiscreet."

Santa looked. Betty and Donald had left. So Santa decided to tell. "He said that he wanted me to bring you and your wife something."

"For me? For us?"

"He wants his parents to be always happy and to be proud of him. Could you do that, Mister?"

It made perfect sense to me. I never understood why this baffled my father.

6

"Slugging and Singing"

I was a model student, performing extremely well in kindergarten. On the way to play T-ball with the boys in my class, I would run through where the girls were jumping rope, and I would jump the rope perfectly with a stylized dance step. I could bat well and throw well; catching the ball took a little more practice, but Dad made time to practice with me, to sharpen my skills. Sometimes, Dad would call me "Slugger. " To Dad, my athleticism proved to be the most important thing about the kindergarten years - to prove my "manhood," I guess. Hindsight is the Monday morning quarterback or something like that.

When I entered kindergarten, it was the age of the "smiley face." Mom was more concerned with seeing this little symbol appear on my papers and I did not disappoint her. And I was not antisocial when called to do something in class with a group. But my playtime memories were those of being a loner with no specific friends - of either gender.

This was also the age when parents attended parent conferences religiously. And my parents were among the most religious. “All of Donald's grades are more than satisfactory,” my teacher told them. “As a colleague, Mrs. Danforth, you must have sensed how intelligent Donald is.”

Mom nodded. “Yes. But a parent is never certain if it is her own prejudice - “

“In Donald's case,” my teacher interrupted, “there is no question. His reading readiness, the fundamentals of mathematics - “

“All these things are high normal,” added the school counselor. “It is our job to look at the whole child. So, we thought we could take this opportunity to talk about Donald's behavior.”

Dad was concerned. “He's not causing you any problems, is he? We weren't aware - “

My teacher saw where this was going. “His behavior in class is just fine.”

“It's not the way Donald relates to other children,” explained the counselor. “It’s the way that other students relate to him.” And there was a long pause.

My mother asked, “Meaning?”

“It could not have escaped your attention that Donald is, well, a loner. It’s normal for some children to be standoffish when school starts as they adjust."

Mom didn't understand what the fuss was about. "He's just a child. Our little boy - "

For some reason, my Dad said, "I can guarantee you that his interests are, well, male."

Ignoring this, the counselor asked, "Could it be that Donald has no brothers or sisters? Neighborhood playmates?"

"I never gave it much thought," my father responded. "He spends most of his time with us."

The counselor explains, "We need to know these things so that we can make school a more pleasant experience for Donald."

Dad shrugged. “I wasn't under the impression that Donald found school unpleasant.”

My teacher assured my parents, “We want Donald to fit in.”

Mom asked, “You want Donald to conform?”

My teacher began, “I don't think - “

Dad interrupted, “Well, that's obvious.”

Sensing the increase in tension, my teacher said, “Let's be calm, please.” She tried to explain. “Here's an example. When the children pick teams, none of the boys choose Donald.”

Dad asked, “Are you saying that Donald is not liked by the other children?”

My teacher answered, “No, of course not.”

The counselor added, “Most of the children have their own groups, friends with whom they identify and play.” Turning to my mother directly, she said, “As a teacher, you know this.”

Mom looked into my teacher’s eyes. “You say the boys never select Donald.”

My teacher nodded. “But the girls don't associate with Donald either. At first, I wondered if it were because Donald can jump rope better, dance better. Donald is more graceful than any of the girls.”

Mom asked, “How can ‘grace’ be a problem? What about Rudolph Nureyev?”

The counselor was confused. “The

ballet dancer?"

As was my teacher. "What has that got to do with - "

Mother pressed on. "Rudolph Nureyev, Alexander Gudonov, Barishnikov - they're graceful men. Gregory Hines? I wouldn't think their grace made them unpopular."

And Dad backed her up. "Quite the contrary."

Mom continued. "They are male dancers who are graceful and successful, some of the best athletes - "

The counselor broke in. "So you are suggesting that Donald would adjust well if we allowed him to dance?"

Betty pressed on. "Dancers, like

athletes, are team players. I’m suggesting that being graceful does not mean that he will always be a loner. That's his choice.”

My teacher said, “We’re not accusing Donald of being abnormal by any means.”

Dad said firmly, “I should hope not.”

The counselor added, “And even if he were abnormal, the public school system should accommodate - “

Dad stood and spoke more loudly. “Donald is not abnormal. For Christ's sake, why are we having this discussion? Donald is five years old.”

My teachers tried to calm my father. “I think we have a solution here.”

Dad was still near to shouting. “What?”

“We'll have a Christmas pageant in about six weeks. I think giving Donald an opportunity to perform could give all that ‘grace’ and athleticism an outlet.”Mom softened. “You do?”My teacher nodded. “Let us try.”

As if it were yesterday, I can see children assembled in the "cafetorium" preparing for the Christmas pageant. Who was it that said: “There
are no small parts - only small actors”? Well, the cafetorium was full of them. All the actors were to be stars for their parents; none of them felt rehearsal was necessary.

My teacher silences the group. “So today, we’re going to assign roles for our Christmas pageant.” She passed out cards, not scripts, which explained what each of the children was to do.

"Eric will play Santa." Eric, an overweight boy, accepted his role.

"Michelle will play Mary." Michelle, a pretty little girl, accepted her role.

"Sam will play Joseph." Sam, tall and slender for five, accepted his role.

And then my teacher bestowed my part upon me. "Donald will play the Sugar Plum Fairy."

I was miffed. "The Sugar Plum Fairy?"

If my teacher knew that I was miffed, she gave no sign. "Yes, Donald. We need an excellent dancer to play the Sugar Plum Fairy. We've even brought in a ballet teacher to choreograph your role."

I had a solution. "Couldn't I just play an angel?"

"No," my teacher disagreed pleasantly, "and this is Miss Heasman, your choreographer. Go with her."

I shrugged and went with Miss Heasman, a waifish white woman, blonde, who had a smile like the beam of a lighthouse. She took my hand, and we went to the back of the room as I heard my teacher proclaim: "Melina will play Rudolph the Red Nosed Reindeer." Melina had a cold and a red nose and blew her nose. Also, "Taurus will play Frosty the Snowman." Taurus was a very dark, cheerful, chubby child. Finally, "And

Gerald will play Round John Virgin." Gerald was a sweet-faced child. All these were great roles and I felt much better suited to them than "the Sugar Plum Fairy."

Miss Heasman asked me, "Have you ever danced before?"

I shrugged my shoulders in the universal childhood gesture. "Everybody dances."

"Have you ever taken dancing lessons?"

"No. I never really wanted to."

"Well, we won't do anything hard. The piece of music is short. I brought it on tape so you can hear it." Miss Heasman brought out a tape player and played "The Dance of the Sugar Plum Fairy" from The

Nutcracker. I listened and didn’t like what I heard. “What's the matter?”

I frowned. “It’s so slow.”

“Yes.”

“If I dance to something slow, something like that, they'll laugh.”

“And that would ruin your performance, huh?”

I looked in my teacher’s direction. “Maybe it’s not too late for me to be a shepherd.”

Undaunted, Miss Heasman asked, “How about this?” and played "The Russian Dance" from The Nutcracker. Now, this was more like it!

I nodded my head to the rhythm. “That's cool!”

"What if you danced to that?" she asked. I grinned sweetly at her. "I like."

I rehearsed with Miss Heasman until I got the dance down pat. At the dress rehearsal, I performed the dance perfectly on the stage until the final leap. The stage was not big enough and I went sailing off the stage.

We arrived for the Christmas program; I was on crutches, and my ankle was broken.

My teacher greeted us. "We're so sorry about Donald's accident, but he can perform with the choir." She took me to the choir while my parents found seats.

Dad took out his camera as he watched me get situated on the stage. "At least the crutches put him on the front row."

Mom said, "Get lots of pictures."

After Santa arrived, the principal took the stage. "At this point in our pageant, as you will see in your programs, Donald Danforth was to perform 'The Dance of the Sugar Plum Fairy,' but unfortunately, Donald broke his foot. So, at this point of the program, instead, the Kindergarten Choir will sing 'Oh, Come All Ye Faithful.'"

The parents applauded. My teacher urged, "Remember children, sing loud."

But when the rest began to sing, they were barely audible over the piano. I was uncomfortable
since I was unrehearsed.

"Oh, come all ye faithful, joyful and

triumphant"

My teacher mouthed, “Louder, children.”

"Oh, come ye. Oh, come ye. To Bethlehem."

Then she pleaded, “Please, somebody please sing louder.”

I didn’t know how else to sing it louder other than to sing at the top of my lungs in the style of Lady Soul, Aretha Franklin:

"Come and behold him. Born the king of angels.

Oh, come let us behold him.

Oh, come let us behold him.

Oh, come let us behold him. Christ the Lord!"

And I continued the song. The spotlights kept me from seeing that all the other parents' mouths were open as were most of the kids. Mom and Dad were proud. I just thought that I was singing the way I was supposed to be singing. Wasn't I?

7

“Turning Twelve!”

By the time that I was twelve, I did a lot of day-dreaming in the dark. I would let my imagination fly, early in the morning before the rest of the world was awake. It was still dark when birds began to sing. They knew something was coming. I wanted to be tuned into the world that way.

Of the seasons, I remember loving autumn most of all. I would lie on my back in a pile of leaves looking at some clouds floating by. Or I would look at my wristwatch and have thoughts about time: Was it a constant? Was it a fiction? I was never bored so time didn't slow down for me; immersing me in music did seem to make time speed up. What was it King Mongkut said? "It is a puzzlement"?

Twelve is the point at which I first gave serious thought to my gender. Well, I did walk with the vaguest hint of a swish, but it wasn't overt. I didn't walk a lot, anyway. "There goes Donald on his bicycle," I'd hear people say. My bike and I were best friends.

I rode my bike to school, a new middle school, to begin the sixth grade. I parked my bike and remember both boys and girls staring at me. Then again, most kids at that age are self-conscious. And most kids also stare at other kids.

This is the first time that I had a home room. Many of the kids there were kids that I had been with in elementary school, but they were changing.

The home room teacher explained, " . . . the Junior 4H is for students who have an interest in agriculture and farm animals. Are there any questions?"

I asked, “Did you mention choir?”

A boy whose name I didn’t know said cockily, “Donald's a soprano.” I didn’t look at him, refusing to dignify his jab, but other students responded with nervous laughter.

The teacher said, “Oh, don't be silly,” to him. Then to me, she said, “No, Donald, I'm afraid the school board has cut back funds for the arts and middle school athletics this year, so there is no choir.”

With a mock effeminate voice, the same kid said: “There's still a home economics club,” which was met with more nervous laughter.

The teacher suggested something that I wasn’t familiar with. “How about the Pop Club?” That was a club where students, mostly girls, would dance to popular music.

I adjusted. I found physical education frustrating because some of the boys made a joke of consistently seeking me out in the locker room or showers to “make sure” that I had my genitalia. I did join the drama club, but although I felt I was the most capable boy in the class, casting me seemed to be a problem. As always, I had good grades, but I was not comfortable socially. When I would pick a place to sit at lunch with the rest of the guys, the guys got up and moved elsewhere. When I worked up my courage to sit by a cute girl, she would say: "I'm sorry. This seat is taken."

So rather than making friends in middle school, my friends were the clouds.

And my friends were soul records. And my friends were blues records. And my anthem was Louis Prima's "I Ain't Got Nobody." And before I knew it, middle school was over. And I felt ankle-deep in the registration paperwork from the high school.

Mom looked at the lists of courses on the registration form. “Oh, now, that looks like fun. Mixed choir?”

I shrugged. “I'm not really interested in choir anymore.”

Mom gave me one of those suspicious looks that moms the world over are famous for. “But you were always disappointed that the middle school didn't have a choir. The high school choir makes lots of trips. Why, last year, they went to the national finals at

Disney World. They stayed gone for a week. Doesn't that sound like fun?"

To which I responded, "Not for a boy whose voice hasn't changed."

Sympathetic, Mom reasoned, "Oh, Donald, they need boys with high voices. Tenors are absolutely essential to an award winning choir. Lots of famous guys are tenors. Johnny Mathis?"

This singer had somehow escaped our record collection: "Johnny who?"

Mom tried another singer that she knew I liked. "What about David Ruffin? You like the Temptations."

I shook my head. "Mom, that's falsetto. My voice is - "What should I have called it? " - well, 'real-setto.'"

Undaunted, Mom continued, “Some of the truly great progressive rock singers have voices that are ‘real-setto.’ Jon Anderson? Roger Daltry?”

I shook my head again. “They're great, but they're white. The closest voice to mine is that new girl, Mariah Carey.”

This frustrated Mom’s attempts. “Okay. Forget choir for now. Maybe band is for you. What courses do you have down so far?”

“Just core courses, Mom,” I said. “English, algebra, physical science,” and with disgust, “P.E.”

Dad came into the house after a hard day at the office. That’s what he said. He never seemed to me to have a hard day at the office. What was hard about insurance? Looking back on it, I think I was hard on my Dad when I was in high school. But he did say stupid stuff like “I'm home!” He kissed Mom and ruffed my hair which seemed to me to be a particularly white dad thing to do, but then he tried to fix it by saying the “hippest” thing he knew: “What's up?”

Mom explained chirpily. “Donald got his registration materials for high school today.”

“Dad, do I have to take P.E.?”

Mom interceded. “Donald, everybody has to take P.E.”

Siding with me, sort of, Dad said, “Not if you go out for a sport. Then, they wave P.E., and you get a study hall.”

Swapping one hell for another, I thought.

Mom prodded me. “I don’t see why you don't just take P.E.”

“Because I feel funny about the dressing out part.”

Dad rubbed the back of his neck. “You'd have to dress out for a sport, too. Let's see what sports are available?” Dad picked up the sheet of
paper. “Ah! Freshman football - “

“Football?” I protested. “Just what I need. To be tackled by some jocks. They'd kill me!”

Dad continued to read. “basketball, soccer, track, and squash. Squash?”

I lay my head on the table, covering

my eyes. “That's for girls.”

Dad looked more closely. “So it is. Hmm. No tennis? No golf?”

I shook my head. “Nope.”

“That's a shame,” said Dad. “I could have helped coach you in tennis or golf.” A long silence was followed by “Well, son, if you don't want to take P.E., and you don't want physical contact, then, it looks like track. In the fall, it meets at the same time as football, so your path won't cross with that particular group of jocks.”

I knew there were no more options. “Okay.”

Mom circled track. “I'm glad that's taken care of. What's left?”

“I have an interest check list,” I

explained, “and they'll assign me to some mini-courses based on the interests that I select.”

“Well, be sure to pick philatelic studies,” my Dad said to Mom while I searched the sheet for the topic. “Nothing brings a father and son together like working on a stamp collection!”

Thank God, that was over. “How about football?” I asked, getting the ball. “Would you pass a few to me, Dad?”

Dad smiled, loosening his tie. We went out into the front yard to play. I wondered if he saw the irony.

The next day after a marathon bike-riding and thinking session, I came into the kitchen. Mom was there. Max, our cat, was there. Max had something to do with Mother’s love for the Andrew Lloyd Webber - T.S. Eliot musical. She asked, “Everything go okay at school?”

I shrugged. “Business as usual.”

Mom tried not to read too much into this. “You get all your high school registration materials turned in?”

“Yes, Mom.”

“Say, feed the cat, will you?” she asked.

“Sure. Come here, Max.” I opened a can, put it in a bowl, and pet the cat. Then, I treated Max to some fresh water.

“Say,” she added. “I volunteered you for something today. I hope you don't mind.”

I rolled my eyes. “What now?”

“The church is having this thing called ‘Hamburgers for the Homeless.’ Instead of a soup kitchen, this Saturday they’re grilling out hamburgers. And since you enjoy flipping burgers when Dad cooks out, I thought you'd enjoy doing it for the church.”

“You could have asked me first,” I said.

Mom placed her hands on my shoulders and looked into my eyes. “And you would have said?”

“Yes,” I grinned.

A few days later, I remember Dad bringing in an envelope from the mail box - from the school system - addressed “to the parents of Donald Danforth." Dad opened it and read aloud to the entire world: "'Advanced English, advanced algebra, band and orchestra, advanced physical science, track, sewing and costume design, hair care, gourmet cooking?' What the hell?"

Mom was concerned about Dad's reaction.

"What?"

Dad was furious about something. "They've got Donald signed up for sewing and costume design, hair care, and gourmet cooking."

Mom shrugged. "Could it be a mistake?"

Dad found the work sheet that I had

prepared by hand before filling out the coded registration. “No. Here's the sheet Donald filled out. It's in his handwriting. Donald chose sewing and costume design, hair care, and gourmet cooking. Those are his interests.”

“Well, that's okay isn't it?”

Dad was hesitant. “Maybe.”

Mom studied him. “What's wrong?”

“I'm worried about Donald, Betty.”

“Donald?”

“He's a great son; don't get me wrong. He does well in school. He's a wonderful kid. But sometimes I notice, maybe through a gesture or a step, well - “Mom gave Dad a hard look. “Betty, I love Donald, and he'll always be my son. But haven't you noticed that he's effeminate?"

Mom spoke harshly. "You think Donald is effeminate simply because he wants to take sewing and costume design, hair care, and gourmet cooking?"

Dad held up the registration confirmation. "Well, it's that added to everything else - "

Mom tried to reason with him. "The tailor who makes your suits is a man; Bill. The barber who cuts your hair is a man, Bill. The master chef at your favorite restaurant is a man, Bill. Don't assume that your son is not a man!" As I listened to my parents discuss this, well, you can imagine how it made me feel. This home was my safe haven, yet the footing was far from firm.

Saturday afternoon came, and I was grilling burgers. The church was playing lively gospel music, soulful and with a rocking beat, Albertina Walker comes to mind, so I cooked the burgers with rhythm - almost dancing. People gathered around and clap to the rhythm which got me even more into the act. Several church people commented on my dance routine, but a homeless man said: "That kid sure can cook

I was still flipping burgers to songs like "Shake Your Groove Thing." When the music stopped, I served up my last bunch of burgers while admirers applauded my dancing and my culinary expertise. I responded with a huge smile until one of the homeless men approached me, winking.

"You cook a fine hamburger, cutie."

At church, too? I thought, irritated. "I'm not a cutie. I'm a boy."

The homeless man looked at me with dismay. What was he thinking? Should I have cared what other people thought?

I rode back to the park on my bicycle to my safe haven where I would make myself the companion of the clouds. And among my companions, my anger turned into a tear.

After a while, I rode my bike home and Mom met me at the back door. "Donald, what happened? We thought you'd be home hours ago."

I must have appeared sullen. "I was at the park."

"For three hours?"

"I had to sort some things out."

Dad echoed Mom. "For three hours?"

I knew that I'd might as well cut to the chase. "A man at the cookout. He called me a cutie."

Mom did not follow the shift well. "What does that mean?"

I continued. "And he winked at me. Like he wanted to pick me up or something."

Dad was quicker. "Come in, son. Sit down." We went into the den. I sat down. Dad turned at the door and spoke to Mom. "Betty, I want to talk to Donald alone, all right? Father to son."

Mom was used to being a buffer.

"Bill - "

"Betty, please." Mom obviously did not want to leave the conversation, but she did. Dad put his hand on my shoulder and looked into my eyes. "Did this man who winked at you, did he touch you?"

"No."

"I'm sorry that this happened; your mom and I thought the cookout would be fun."

"The cookout was great. I flipped burgers. We fed over a hundred people. I mean, people even applauded when I flipped the burgers. It felt great. And then, some guy acted like he wanted to - " To what? Was I even sure what he wanted from me? " - and it all fell apart."

"I see."

"Do you?" What I had built up inside of me had been coming for a long time. "Dad, I have no friends, but that's okay. The guys don't like me but that's okay. Girls don't like me but that's okay. I don't get it, but that's okay. Then, some guy acts like he's flirting with me in the park."

"Son, I've noticed that you're - maybe slightly - effeminate. When you say that you want to take sewing and costume design, hair care, and gourmet cooking - "

"So you think what, Dad?"

"You know I love you, Donald. And I would still love you, no matter what."

I resorted to the universal sign that kids employ when their parents just don't get it: I rolled my eyes. "No matter what?

What does that mean: ‘No matter what‘?” Dad didn’t immediately answer, so I shot out the door, got on my bicycle and was gone before I could hear their conversation, out on the driveway.

Dad asked, “Should we get in the car and follow him?”

Mom, still displeased with not being included in Dad’s conversation with me asked, “What did you say?”

“I wanted to reassure him that I still love him.”

“That you still love him? Are you nuts? How did you think he'd take that, that you ‘still love him‘? He hasn't done anything wrong. He’s a child, Bill. You're annoyed by his mini-course choices, and you think he's effeminate. What if he's gay?"

Dad tried to make his point. "I hope not, but if he is, I still love him."

"Don't follow him. I would think that you are the last person that he wants to see right now. If
he needs anyone to believe in him, it's you."

"Look, he's coming back."

But I wasn't. I was merely whizzing by on my bicycle, not turning into the driveway. I kept on going but with nowhere to go. I was merely circling the block.

Always astute, I heard Dad remark, "He's going in circles."

"Can you blame him? We're his only friends, but he can't come here now because his father thinks he's effeminate."

"He is!" Dad protested. "But I only said that - "

I didn't hear the end of that sentence, but it didn't matter. I knew what he had said. I kept circling the block. Mom and Dad kept watching from the driveway. I had nowhere else that I wanted to go, but I wasn't ready to go home, either. In my head, I started to hear Chuck Berry's "No Particular Place to Go," and I fell into that rhythm while peddling.

Later, I heard Dad ask Mom on one of my passes, "How many now?"

I count sixty-eight. He's not slowing down."

"Do you think it's me?"

Mom gave him a hard look. "Yes."

"Maybe, if I go inside, he'll be more likely to come home. "

"Maybe."

"So, I think I'll do that, then."

"Yes. Go hide. I don't want him to see you even if I get him back inside the house." And then she said more to herself than to Dad, "He'll be circling the block all night."

Dad watched one more pass. "Well, all right." He went in the house. I continued circling a couple of more times. Then, Mom went into the kitchen and puttered around. Seeing no one in my driveway, I pulled my bike into the garage and parked it. I went gingerly into the kitchen.

Mom didn’t look at me, but said: “You're back.”

“Yeah.” I tried to think of something to say; the cat rubbed up against the back of my legs. “I see you still have the same cat.”

Mom tried not to laugh. “Yeah.”

“I'm not effeminate.”

Mom tried to think of some kind of slam-dunk encouragement. “I remember changing your diapers. Ain't nothing feminine about you, kid.”

“And I like girls. I think about girls a lot.” How does one speak of such things in front of one’s mother. “I want to be with girls.”

“I believe you.”

“I mean, I know I’m different. But

you taught me that everybody is different." I tried my best to make this sound like an affirmation and not an accusation.

"Everybody is, honey. It's just that in the way that you are different, sometimes people jump to conclusions and think the wrong things."

"Even Dad?"

Dad's not perfect. But you need to understand your father. He's a lot like you, really. All his life, some people have misunderstood his drive to succeed and be the best at his profession: Because of the way he speaks and dresses and because he is smart and successful, they think he's trying to be white."

"Is he?"

"Of course not. He's trying to be himself. Just as you are trying to be yourself. But because Dad was trying so hard to be himself, he made a mistake and has been trying to compensate for it by being understanding when what he was trying to understand was himself - not who or what you are. Does that make sense to you?"

Not completely. So I responded, "Sort of."

"Having an identity all your own isn't easy. There was a time when we were told that we 'had a place.' It was like there were little pigeonholes for everybody and we were supposed to go hide in ours. That day has passed for what even my mama used to call colored people. Because we stood up as a group, we were heard and now we can be ourselves. But the day has not come yet that an individual like you can be an individual. Perhaps by the time you are grown, you can be yourself and no one will shun you for it. But that time isn't yet. And it may be hard for you for a while yet." Mom put her arms around me and held me tightly. "But I'm here for you, Donald. Whatever you are, you are my son, and you are not effeminate. And accept that."

I'm glad she couldn't see the look on my face when she said "whatever you are." But I understood what she was trying to say. "Thanks, Mom."

"Be patient with your father, Donald. He's a good man."

“I know. I wish I were what he wants”

“You are. He just hasn't learned that yet - on the outside, but deep inside, I think he knows.”

“Okay.”

“He really loves you, you know.”

“Yeah.”

“And he supports you, no matter what.”

That “no matter what“ phrase had a loud ring of familiarity. “You heard that?”

She released me from her embrace, smiling. “Yes; just because I wasn't in the room, it doesn't mean that I wasn't listening at the door.”

I returned her smile. “Why, you snoop!”

“It's what we women do. It's part of the package.”

“So guess you heard all of that - “

“Most of it.”

“Including the ‘no matter what’?”

Mom nodded. “It’s just that what he thought might have been the 'no matter what,’ wasn't it?” The phrasing was odd, but I didn‘t want to let on that I wasn‘t quite sure what she meant. Then she asked: “Understand?”

I giggled. “Yeah.” I just wish I knew what the "no matter what" is. This would be a lot easier.

After that, I went back to my parents’ bedroom. It was dark. “Dad? You awake?”

“Yes.”

“I'm sorry, Dad.”

“I'm the one who should be sorry, son. I worry about you because you're the only kid that I’ve ever had.”

I sat by him. “No, you'd worry about me even if there were a dozen of us.”

Dad laughed. “You know, when I

was a kid, I used to spend the night with a friend named Gary who had six brothers and six sisters.”

“Yeah?”

“Yeah. His last name was Baker, and no lie, they used to call those kids ‘the Bakers' dozen.’"

“Really?”

He nodded. “They had two huge

dorm-like bedrooms on both sides of the hall, one for the girls and one for the boys, and the youngest boy and the youngest girl, Lester and Leslie, were twins, right?"

"Right."

"And they had little chirpy voices like tree frogs.

I giggled. Kids who talked like tree frogs? Anything that would relieve tension was welcome.

"So at night," Dad continued, "the parents might call for one of the older kids or another, and the twins would check, and usually call back:" and he mimicked them with a high, squeaky voice,

"'She 'sleep" or "He 'sleep!'"

"'He 'sleep'"?

“Yeah.” Dad laughed again. “Not ‘She's asleep’ or ‘He's asleep’ but ‘He 'sleep!’"

Just the thought now had me convulsed with laughter.

“One night, Gary's father and mother started calling all of them. It sounded like a chorus of little frogs. ‘He 'sleep!’ ‘She 'sleep!’ ‘He 'sleep!’ ‘She' sleep!’ ‘He 'sleep!’ ‘She 'sleep!’"

And we both hugged one another, laughing so hard? That was the last I remember.

8

"Angela"

I had told you that I was a loner as a kid. That was true until I met Angela. I was in the school cafeteria enjoying my lunch about as much as my other high school classmates, seated alone as usual. I didn't see the pretty girl approaching but approach she did.

"This seat taken?"

I figured that she was just another annoyance, someone who had been dared to sit by me as some sort of initiation. I shrugged and shook my head. She sat down.

"Why are you sitting by yourself? All the cool kids are sitting over there." She pointed to a table where the obvious high school elite were seated.

"That's why I'm not over there. I'm not one of them."

The pretty girl started to eat. "Well, I thought you were one of the cool kids. You sure are good looking."

I made a scoffing noise. You know, something between "harumph" and "huh." "Those guys think I'm gay."

The pretty girl shrugged. "So?" I looked away; the pretty girl pointed. "You could sit over there with all the gay kids. See?"

I shook my head. "But I'm not gay."

The pretty girl thought for a second. Then she smiled sweetly. "Okay."

I looked her in the eye. "What do you mean, 'okay'?"

"I mean 'okay' that I believe you. That you're not gay." She offered me her hand. "I'm Angela."

I took it. "I'm Donald."

Angela smiled and continues to eat. I

looked at her inquisitively. Then I smiled, too.

Angela and I did everything together. Three
years of high school passed quickly and happily. We were best friends. And since neither of us were dating anyone, I took Angela to the prom. I arrived at her house, put a corsage on her and drove to the Chattanooga Garden Inn in my dad's Caprice. "I've never seen you smile like this. I thought you said that prom wasn't that big a deal."

"Are you kidding? We're seniors. We've survived high school. This is our only senior prom." She laughed. "It's not a big deal at all. It's just that I have a surprise for you later."

"A surprise? What is it?"

"If I told you, it wouldn't be a surprise, now would it?"

Of course, Angela and I were not king and queen of the prom. That would have seemed too "Carrie." But we had a wonderful time. The DJ played "Love Hangover" and couples took turns dancing. When Angela and I came onto the floor, Angela backed off and let me "cook." Even the kids who had always rejected me had to admit that I was a phenomenal dancer. Well, I was.

Angela and I walked out hand in hand; Angela seemed to be a little tipsy. But I was still on top of the world, so I didn't think much of it. "I can't believe it. This was the greatest surprise. All those kids who - well, I thought they hated me, but when I danced? Well, I guess they don't."

"You were phenomenal!" she shouted. "But that's NOT the surprise."

"What could be better than that?"

She giggled. "Turn around." So I did. Angela put a blindfold on me.

"What's the blindfold for?"

"It's part of the surprise!"

I had never enjoyed being out of control. "I don't like this."

"Don't you trust me?"

"Of course, I do," I said. "You're my best friend."

I heard the whisper of a giggle as

Angela pressed a button and the elevator doors opened. She led me in. “Then, go with it, Donald, and enjoy your surprise.
The elevator doors closed; I sensed Angela push another button. Soon, we were on another floor and I walked zombie-like, led by Angela. A door opened into a hotel room. I smelled a strong odor of flowers.

“Can I take the blindfold off now?” I asked. “I really want to - “

But she wouldn’t let me finish. “No. Now, I’m going to seat you in a chair. And then I’m going to tell you when to take the blindfold off. Not much longer, okay?”

I sat and hesitantly answered: “Okay.” I was curious to hear “Let’s Get It On” coming from a boom box.

"Okay, Donald. I'm going to light some candles, but you can take off your blindfold now." I took off the blindfold. Angela was skipping around the room and started lighting candles. I was
appalled to see that she was wearing a bustierre.

"Angela, what are you doing?"

"I'm lighting candles, silly."

Then, Angela poured two glasses of champagne. She brought one to me, but I didn't take it. She placed it on a table. She jumped on the bed, reclining.

"Angela, what are you doing?"

Angela sang, "I'm gonna give you my cherry." I looked at her as if she'd spoken to me in Swahili. "We are gonna make love.” She pointed at a video camera. “And I brought a camera to record it, see? That way, if anybody calls you a fag, ever again, you have documented proof!”

“Angela, I can’t do this.”

“Don’t you love me?”

“Well, yes, but - “

“It’s been years, Donald. We’ve been together years. It’s time! You tell me that I’m beautiful. Let’s get it on!”

“Angela, you are beautiful, but you are my best friend. I can’t do this! It would be like - well - doing it with my sister.”

Angela got up off the bed and put a passionate kiss on my mouth. I did not pull away, but my response was best called “neutral.” Angela slid her hand down

toward my crotch. I pulled away from her before she could reach my junk. "So
this is how it's gonna be? I offer myself to you, my most precious - " She gestured at her body making sure that I was looking at her. "And you don't want it?"
I didn't know what to say or do. I hung my head. "Well, I guess you are a fag. All this time, you've been lying to me!" Angela got her dress and began to put it back on. "Look at all the trouble I went to, and you don't even want me."

"Angela, you're my best friend!"

"Get out!" she screamed. "Can't you see? A lady's dressing! Get out! You make me sick! Faggot! Get out!"
So I left Angela looking around at the ruin

of her "surprise," grabbing the bottle of champagne and guzzling it.

My eyes glistening, I sat in my father's car unclear as to what to do. Soon, I heard noise in the parking garage. Four large boys in formal wear were with Angela who was VERY drunk. She carried her almost empty champagne bottle and sang, slurring her words: "People all over the world: Join hands, and start a love train, love train." Angela frowned and turned to her companions. "You're not singing."
The boys laughed lasciviously.

Knowing this was trouble, I got out of the car, closed the door which resulted in a loud echo, and stepped towards Angela.

"Angela, get in the car, now."

"I don't take orders from you, fag. The O'Jays here and I are going back to - " She thought, lost in a champagne haze. " - somewhere, and we're gonna " She returned to singing. " party!"

Her quartet of boys laughed. One said: "Yay-yah!"

I tried to ignore her entourage. "Angela, right now!"

Another of the boys put a hand on me, pushing me back.

"She comin' with us, little nigga."

Angela echoed: "Yeah, little nigga."

But I stood my ground. "She came with me. She's my date. I picked her up at her house. And now, I'm taking her home."

They challenged me. "She wants to go with us, us real men."

"Out of the way, before we mop up this garage with your ass."

I replied, as coldly as I knew how: "You probably will, if you decide to. I can't beat up one of you guys, let alone four. But once you've beaten me to a pulp, I'm still taking Angela home."

There is a long pause as the four big guys checked me, the "little nigga" standing his ground. Angela stood still, embracing the champagne bottle. The four big guys all looked at each other; it would have been funny had I not been scared to death. I guess I hid it well because against what I was expecting, the four guys walked away.

Before she could object, I took Angela's arm and put her in the car.

The next day, I should have been sleeping, but instead, I lay on my bed. The phone rang. I answered. "Donald, it's Angela." I could think of nothing to say; I just listened. "Donald, I'm so sorry. I mean, like, I felt so rejected and I should never drink champagne, but I said some things that I didn't mean. Donald?" But I did not respond. "Donald, can you forgive me? Donald?"

Dad entered my room. Seeing me on the phone, he said: "Oh, I'm sorry. I thought - "

I hung up the phone. "It's okay, Dad. That was nobody."

Dad said, "Paul Maples came by the agency. Looks like he was impressed enough by your math scores to give you that summer job at the bank. Put aside a little spending money for college?"

"Yeah, Dad, sure. Thanks."

Dad gave me a thumbs-up sign.

"Dad, when do I begin?"

"Monday morning. 8 a.m. Sharp."

9

“Working, Atlanta, and Rita”

Monday morning came and there I was at the bank in a crisp French blue shirt and a white tie, standing at my teller window along with four pretty but middle aged ladies standing at theirs. Just before the bank opened, a nattily dressed balding man, Paul Maples, strutted past the tellers on the way to his office. I wondered: Should I thank him now or later in a more private setting for giving me this opportunity?

Mr. Maples touched the brim of his fedora. “Good morning, ladies.”

I knew that he had looked directly at me. I frowned. One of the tellers noticed. Was this an insult? The others said at various cadences “Good morning, Mr. Maples.”

The first teller decided to correct this misunderstanding. “Oh, Mr. Maples? Donald is starting today.”

Maples removed his hat and looked at me. Was he trying to be funny? “As I said, good morning, ladies. ”Chuckling, Maples went into his office.

I placed the “Window Closed” sign on my window. I walked out of the bank past the incoming customers.

I walked into Frank’s Diner, a traditional lunch counter in old Chattanooga. I ordered a cup of coffee. I saw the help wanted sign. The waitress brought me a cup and poured the amber hot and delicious liquid. I asked: “What kind of help do you need?”

Her name was Wanda; she looked at me with surprise. “Short order cook for lunch and evening.” I smiled at her and she continued. “Pay’s terrible and it’s a lonely job.”

"What do you mean, 'lonely'?"

Wanda cocked her head toward the kitchen.

"You work by yourself back there. Nobody wants to"

"Minimum wage?"

"You guessed it."

I took down the sign and handed it to the waitress. "I'm your man."

And that's how I became the short order cook at Frank's Diner. For a while.

I thought things were going to work out for me at U.T. Chattanooga. I was in the dorm, still studying my orientation materials when there was a knock at my door. Three gay men were at the door when I opened it; they walked right in.

One said, “Hi! I’m Jade and this is Cynthia and this is Dave. We came to welcome you to the campus.”

“Oh? Do you do this for all freshmen?” I asked.

The man called “Cynthia” responded. “Oh, no. We did this because you’re one of us.”

“What do you mean, ‘one of us‘?”

“As in gay.”

“As in gay? I need to inform you that I’m not gay, and I’m offended by this, and I want you to leave my damn room.”

Shocked, my welcoming committee left. I picked up the phone and punched my home number. Mom answered. “Hello?”

“Mom. I’ve gone through twelve

years of this madness."

"What do you mean?"

"You know what I mean! I'll be damned if I can take four more years of it. And I'm not really about this college thing, anyway."

"Now, Donald, to get ahead in this world, you need a college education."

"I'll be withdrawing from all my classes first thing in the morning. I'm out of here. And I'm not coming home."

"But Donald, no; where are you going?"

"I love you, Mom. Tell Dad I love him. I'll let you know where I am when I get there."

The next day, I was greeted by the

Atlanta skyline. I was driving the new sub-compact that my parents had given me for graduation. I pulled into a used car lot, and after a little haggling, I walked away with a pocketful of money. I used some of my money for the deposit and first payment on an efficiency apartment. I put my things away. I looks out the window to see if I could see much of Atlanta from the window. I couldn't. But I did see a sight that intrigued me: The Varsity, an old-fashioned drive-in style restaurant in the heart of Atlanta.

There I was again, working in the kitchen. This place was so busy that I was not alone, but the pace of the place kept me from being bothered by anyone. I cooked on the late night to breakfast shift. One morning near dawn, I was given a large breakfast order. When I finished preparing it, I placed the order on the counter for a waiter to take to the three customers. When the customers, a lesbian and two gay men, saw me, they gave me that all too familiar look. I went back to work. But for some reason, they spoke too loudly to be ignored.

"What have we here, bitches?"

"A transsexual, methinks?"

"Pre-op or post-op."

I glanced back into the dining room. The waiter left the food.

"Maybe even no-op. Could be a mighty pretty boy or my kind of girl?"

"So how do we find out?"

"I know a way." One of the gays called out to their waiter. "I ordered these eggs over easy. But they're too runny. Would you take them back and have the cook prepare them again?"

The waiter nodded and brought the plate back to me. The customer is always right? Well, I cooked more eggs. The waiter returned to the table, and the gay guy sampled the eggs, which I had made absolutely certain were fine. The gay guy made a cartoon-style coughing noise and motioned to the waiter who returned. "Sir?"

"Tell the cook that the eggs are still too fucking runny. Take 'em back."

The waiter shrugged. He brought the eggs back to me. Once again, I prepared the eggs perfectly. I whispered to the waiter. The waiter returned to the table with the eggs, once again perfect. “The cook says if you don’t like the eggs this time, we’ll take‘em off your check but he ain’t cookin’em again.”

“You tell him to say that to my face.”

The waiter came back to me, looked at me sympathetically, and told me. I approached the trio myself.

“Sir - “

“The eggs are fine.”

I must have looked confused.

“You should have come out the first time George complained and saved yourself a lot of trouble.”

The lesbian spoke. “Yeah, baby.

What? You playing hard to get?"

"You said the eggs were - "

"We're drunk. We were just having fun, darling. Sit down!"

"I don't think - "

"He's not hitting on you, honey. We're a committed couple."

"Yes, and unless you got a pussy, you hold no razzle-dazzle for Rita."

Something told me that these three were okay. I spoke to the shift manager. "Randy, all right if I take my break?"

"Sure, kid, you've been rockin' and rollin' all night without one. Almost time to go."

So I sat in the booth with the trio. Before long, we were all laughing hysterically as Rita continued a tale.

" . . . So I told these two that if they ever left Miami that they should come up here to Hot-lanta and paint the town with me. And here they are. And last night? Damn if we didn't paint it RED!"

10

“Rita Educates Me”

Two weeks later, I was finishing my shift. Rita was there waiting for me. Waiting with a coffee to go. She smiled at me. I said, “That makes five times in the last two weeks, Rita. You must be the Varsity's best customer."

"Nope. Just a night owl. But we night owls need our coffee to stay on the prowl."

I took her arm and escorted her out of the Varsity.

"Besides," she said softly. "I think you need a friend."

I said nothing in reply.

"You got anybody?"

I tried to change the subject. "How are George and John?"

"Fine. Back in Miami. I talked to them last night; they send their love." She raised an eyebrow, listening for a response. She got one.

"Rita, I need to tell you something."

Rita raised the other eyebrow.

"I'm not gay."

"Oh, I know."

"Oh? How do you know?"

"Because any time I talk about my lady loves, you never chip in anything about anybody. And if you were DC and not AC, you couldn't help but volunteer some information. It's part of the profile."

"Maybe I'm just shy," I shrugged.

"Shee-it! As pretty as you are, by now, if you wuz a sweet boy, you would have had an army of lovers."

I said, "Hmm." Just "hmm."

"Plus, I didn't feel it in my spirit. Gay or straight, black women feel things in their spirit." Rita weighed her words carefully and then asked: "Have you ever thought about, well, to try dressing like a girl?"

I pulled away from her. "No! And I'm offended that you would suggest - "

"Hey, it doesn't mean that you are gay; we both know you're not. It's just that you'd make such a pretty girl."

"Rita, dammit, I - "

"No offense meant, kiddo, but you need to do something. From where I stand, you're miserable."

Was I miserable? I didn't think of myself as miserable. I thought of myself as mad. Angry with people who judged me from the outside without getting to know me inside. And it was this frustration that I was considering when I came out of a department store loaded down with packages. I got on a bus. A very colorfully dressed black man and his slightly less colorful girlfriend sat on the bus near me. The woman was demure, like a cat. The man looked in my direction, noted that his girlfriend was not paying attention and winked at me! At first, I was not sure that what I saw was a wink, but then, the man blew me a kiss! I stood up and shouted: "What the fuck are you doing, winking at me? Are you gay or something?"

The man's girlfriend looked at the man, quizzically. The man shouted back: "What are you talkin' about, faggot? Ain't nobody winkin' at you!"

I yelled. "The only faggot on this bus is you!" I was ready for a fight but the bus stopped and one of the doors closest to me opened. Suddenly, the bus driver was pushing me off the bus and throwing my packages off behind me. "Why are you throwing me off?"

The bus driver scowled at me. "You started it. I'm finishing it." And the bus driver closed the door.

I gathered my packages and shouted after the departing bus: "Dammit! I didn't start anything. He started it!"

I awkwardly carried my packages and almost ran into two gorgeous women. I wheeled around and looked at them. All I could say was "Wow!"

The girls kept walking. One said to the other, "Now you know we looking fine if we can stop a queer dead in his tracks."

Her companion laughed and asked: "How much did I pay for these jeans?" And she licked her forefinger and touched her finger to her butt and made a sizzling sound. "Worth every cent!"

The two girls slapped a high five and kept walking. Hurt, I held my packages watching them go, my lust turned to bitter disappointment.

Rita opened her door to find me standing outside, solemn - not angry. She said, "Oh, baby! Donald, you look full of woe, as well as wo'e out!"

She let me in and I asked, “What do you want me to do?”

Rita looked at me as if she didn’t quite understand. “Dressing like a girl? Whatever it is, I’ll do it.”

“Are you certain?”

“I guess if I dress like a woman,” I shrugged, “if I am totally convincing as a woman, people will stop calling me a faggot.”

Rita’s eyes sparkled as if she were going into power mode. “All right. I got this! I’ve got some shopping to do. So take a nap. Then, you take a long, soaking bath, a hot one. Relax! You want a joint?”

I never liked drugs. As I told you, I never wanted to be out of control. “No, thanks."

"Just checking. Okay. I'm gone, sugar. Gotta put some strain on my credit cards."

And just like a snap of her fingers, Rita was out the door. I don't remember how long she was gone, but not long before she returned, I decided that I needed a shower. I noted that Rita had a "soap on a rope" - the soap in the shape of a **microphone**. I had given my Dad several soaps on ropes for birthdays and Christmases, usually English Leather. But this was the first microphone I'd seen. Very practical for aspiring shower singers. I was in the second chorus of "Enough Is Enough" when Rita returned.

"I didn't know you could sing like that!" Rita shouted through the crack in the bathroom door.

I shouted in return, "Sister, give me an audience and I'll put on a show!" I wrapped myself in a huge towel and walked in to see boxes and bags all over. How could Rita have carried all that - "What is all of this?"

"I told you, I had this. Are you sure you're ready?"

Exhaling a deep breath, "I'm ready."

Rita did everything to transform me into a "beautiful woman." Beautiful? Me? "The beauty part doesn't take much work but the fashions need alteration." Rita was really fast. I went to the bathroom before I put on the panties and panty hose that completed the ensemble.

"All right, Donald, come out and give me the full effect," Rita called to me. So I came out to show Rita her masterpiece. "Donald, you is drop dead gorgeous! Oh, my God. This is going to be one hell of a night."

I was still a skeptic. "Yeah, right."

Then, Rita brought out a full length mirror. This is the first time I had been able to look at the complete product. Was that me in the mirror? Damn! I could give my own damned self a hard-on! This was totally unexpected. I was ready to conquer the world.

Rita put on her best finery. She had

no modesty; I guess the illusion that she had wrought left me as both one of the girls while at the same time not an object of attraction for her at all. It was about midnight as she looked in the full length mirror at herself, adding the finishing touches. “So, shall we start off at a gay bar?”

“Nigga please!” I said with as much feminine voice as I could muster - and with attitude.

11

"The Heterosex"

The Heterosexual is a night club that lights up downtown Atlanta. It's a jungle of neon. And at one o'clock in the morning, it pulses with the rhythm of the night. Seen at night, it looks like a Mayan pyramid, with neon vines climbing up the side. It had been a Latin club owned by some businessmen, none of whom were Latin. They had named the place La Cucaracha, not realizing that actual Latins would not come to a place called "The Cockroach." It had closed in three months. Some black businessmen who were somewhat mysterious and shadowy had reopened the place as the cutting edge black music establishment in Atlanta. I say shadowy? I don't know that they really were that mysterious, but it led to the mystique of the place. And the name of the place revealed that these guys were straight with a club designed for a straight clientele.

Of course, lesbians were welcome because lesbians appeal to heterosexual men.

Heads turned as Rita and I walked through the place. I was not yet convinced that I was the one turning heads, but I played my role. I had a little trouble negotiating the high heels, but the slow walk made me look even more stately and graceful, glamorous and - yes, mysterious.

A voice called out from the crowd. "Hey, Rita! Who's your friend?"

Rita and I looked at one another. The one thing that we hadn't done is come up with a name for me. A light dawned in Rita's eyes. "This is DeeDee," she said.

A trail of men came up to the table flirting with "DeeDee" and Rita, offering to buy us drinks, asking the "girls" to dance. Twice, I said yes, for moderately fast songs. I wasn't ready to be held by another man. But when I got on the dance floor, I started to see myself as DeeDee. Up until then, I was Donald!"

After dancing, I returned to Rita and said: "I can't remember when I've had so much fun and it's double because I'm kind of like a spy. I've never gotten this much attention!"

Rita looked at me slyly. "Are you sure that this isn't the real you?"

"I don't know yet," I admitted, "but the real me needs to pee."

"All right." Rita stood. "Girls go in pairs."

We got up and headed for the restroom. The men's room was next door to the ladies' room. I almost went into the men's room. Fortunately, Rita yanked me over to the door of the ladies' room.

"I won't feel comfortable in here," I whispered.

Rita whispered, "I guarantee that you'll feel less comfortable in there."

When we returned from the ladies room, I found myself surrounded by admirers and didn't miss Rita as she snuck up to the bandstand to see Artie, the bandleader. She had said, "Hey, Artie."

Rita and Artie had been friends for a long time. "Hey, Rita. How they hangin'?"

Rita grinned. "Artie, you're a laugh

riot." Artie returned the grin; he knew he was funny. "Listen, I have an old girlfriend here with me, and she can sing her ass off."

Artie had heard this before but not from Rita; his response was rehearsed. "And you would like me to call her up to do a little number?"

"Would you?"

Artie always said no, but this was Rita. "For you, Rita, anything."

Rita got back from the bandstand before I knew she was gone. Soon, there was a fanfare played by the band. Artie stepped up to the microphone. "Ladies and gentlemen, we're so happy to have a vocalist in our presence, a young lady who in the review I recently heard, and I quote, 'This girl can sing her ass off!' Would you please make her welcome to the bandstand? **DeeDee**!" Those who thought that they knew who DeeDee was, applauded enthusiastically. Others looked around with a "who the hell is that" look on their faces. What amuses me now looking back on it is that I didn't recognize that they were calling on me! I applauded politely and looked around. Then, I realized that I was "**DeeDee."** I looked at Rita."You said to get you an audience." I rolled my eyes and smiled. I went to the bandstand and whispered to Artie. "Do you know how to play 'One Night Only' from Dream Girls?" I asked. Artie grinned. "Is grits groceries?"

"But not the Dream Girls."

arrangement. The one recorded by Elaine Paige that blends both the slow and fast versions of the song?"

"I've heard it. Just point at me when you want us to kick it into high gear." And that is what I did. I started slow and sultry and I got through a verse and a chorus of the song and then pointed to the band. The band exploded and the lights with it.

And then the audience as well. I expected polite applause, but the audience was in chaos. They were not expecting the performance to be like this.

Artie looked at the crowd. "Oh, my!"

The audience continued to applaud. Rita was jumping up and down. Walking up behind her right shoulder was a man, smartly dressed in an Armani suit. He looked quizzically at me as if to ask: “Where has this girl been all my life?” Close to the bar, he caught the bartender’s eye and they nodded at one another. The sharp-dressed man backed away from Rita. She continued to shout encouragement during my ovation from the crowd. It’s funny that while I was acknowledging the chanting of the crowd - “DeeDee! DeeDee!” - I was able to focus in on the scene. Since Rita was ignoring the man, he went to ask the bartender who I was.

Despite her assurances that she was “100% lesbian,” I found out later that the sharp-dressed man’s name was Eddie and that he used to sleep with Rita. As I came down from the bandstand, I could hear the bartender ask: “Was sleeping with you what turned Rita dyke?” He was not amused. The bartender cocked his head in my direction. “I knew you’d like that if you came in.”

As Eddie moved back to Rita, I felt a hand gently on my arm. Artie was trying to talk me into doing another song. Two men who had been selling drugs in the club sidled up to Eddie.

“Good night for business, boss.”

“Yeah. Who that new gal? She fine! Hoo!”

I was distracted, but I am certain that I heard the sharp-dressed man say, “You never, ever approach me in here, you got that?” after which the two men sheepishly faded back into the crowd.

Mr. Armani suit continued toward Rita. In spite of the noise, I heard him ask her, “Why didn’t you tell me that you went to college?” Rita winked at me as she lied, “You don’t know everything.”

“What was your major?”

“Creative arts. And yours? ‘Doctor of Paraphernalia‘?

But I didn’t hear the rest, as I had agreed to sing Billie Holliday’s “My Man.” Artie was leading me back up the stairs to the bandstand. Damn these shoes!

I sang “My Man” equally well if the reaction of the crowd was any indication. This time, I had put a lot of body language in the song. Eddie was visually moved by my performance. Rita watched Eddie's reaction and found it hilarious since she knew that although she had a long term relationship with Eddie, that deep down, what had separated them was Eddie's homophobia.

I thanked Artie and encouraged the audience to applaud the band. I returned to the table with Rita as the audience went to the floor to dance. Rita was laughing.

I smiled. "What's so funny?" She kept laughing. "Girl, you are never talking me into that again! Don't you ever put me in the spotlight like that."

But she knew that I didn't mean it and we both continued to laugh. I reached for my drink as the bartender arrived at the table with a freshly-opened bottle of the best real French champagne. He poured for Rita and me. DeeDee picks up her glass, confused. Rita gestured with her glass so I looked toward the bar where Eddie, who had the other glass, was toasting us. After draining his glass, Eddie came to the table and got the bartender to refill our glasses. Eddie sat without being asked.

"So Rita, introduce me to your former classmate. I think she must have majored in fine."

A man this polished on the outside but with a line so lame. Rita found the whole thing very amusing.

"Eddie, this is my friend DeeDee."

"Friend?"

"Oh, don't worry about that, Eddie. You have my personal guarantee that there is no one in this room straighter than my friend, here."

The music swelled, so loud that I couldn't be certain what he was saying to me, but I could tell that he was putting his best lines on me, such as they were. I said very little, just smiled nervously. Rita who sipped her champagne and whispered. And I could read her lips: "Oh, Mr. Player-man. Yes, yes, yes. Getting ready to make your play. If you only knew."

12

"Donald or DeeDee"

I'm not certain why it was that when we returned to Rita's place, I was in such a hurry to get out of my DeeDee disguise. But when all was done, I looked in the mirror and saw Donald. When I left the bathroom, breathing a sigh of relief, Rita was lying on her back with that sly smile on her face. I lay down beside her, not in an embrace, but shoulder to shoulder. "Did you see how all the men in that place looked at me?"

"Like starving men at an all-you-can-eat buffet."

"I never had so much fun in all my life."

"Then why not live like this from now on?"

I propped my head up on my forearm. "Because DeeDee is not real, Rita. Donald is real, but DeeDee isn't."

Everybody wears a mask, baby. A facade. On the outside, all of us is what we want the world to see. You know who you really are; so why shouldn't DeeDee be what you let the world see?"

"It was fun! But I couldn't keep it up all the time."

"Why not? Weren't you for once truly happy? Why not?"

First, I said, "Yeah. Why not?" But after thinking, I said, "Here's why not: I can't be DeeDee on my job."

Rita shrugged. "Quit your job."

"I love my job," I objected. "It's something I do well, and it pays the bills."

Rita's phone rang. "I'll bet this is Eddie, wanting to slather some more mac-onnaise on you." I rolled my eyes as Rita answered. "Hello. Do you know what time it is? Oh, hey, Artie."

Rita put the phone between us so I could hear what Artie had to say. "Listen, I need to find a way to get DeeDee to sing - "

Rita smiled at me and said, "I'm afraid I can't do that. What were DeeDee's exact words? 'Girl, you are never talking me into that again! Don't you ever put me in the spotlight like that.'" It was all I could do not to giggle.

"You gotta help me, Rita. She was a sensation. Everybody was talking about her. We want to bring her back for an exclusive engagement, as a headliner."

"A headliner? Well, I'm sort of her agent. She's considering a permanent job in her other passion, the culinary - "

Artie continued: "We'll pay top dollar. Pay her as if she were already a star, but under an exclusive contract, of course."

"Top dollar?" Rita shifted into a business mode that I'd never seen before, taking back the phone. "How much are we talkin' exactly?" She listened. "Six? Well, let me ask her?" Covering the phone, she giggled: "They want DeeDee back for an exclusive contract at the Hetero for a six figure salary. Can the Varsity match that?"

"Can they? Yes. Will they? No. But how are they going to pay me?"

"Weekly, I suppose."

When is not what I meant. "I can't sign checks as DeeDee. DeeDee doesn't exist."

"I'm your manager, if you trust me, they can pay me and I'll pay you."

"And they want me to sing?"

"And dance a little."

I could hear Artie shouting into the phone. "Hello? Hello?"

Rita uncovered the phone. "Yeah. Artie? It took a lot of convincing, but DeeDee will give you a chance. With conditions. Yes, I'll explain all the details when I see you. We'll need a week - "

I shook my head and held up two fingers.

Rita corrected herself. "Two weeks before we start rehearsals. Uh-huh? Tomorrow at four? All right. See you then." Rita hung up the phone and asked me: “Why two weeks?”

“I have to give the Varsity two weeks notice,” I explained.

“The Varsity! Girl, don’t you realize that this will make you rich?”

“Rich?”

“Well, sort of rich. But you’ll be laughing all the way to the bank while you do what you love almost as much as short order cooking while all those men grovel at your feet!”

“You make it sound so, so, fun!”

And Rita and I were laughing again.

I rehearsed for two weeks. Dancing in the heels was rough, but I got used to it. I was taking a break on the last day of rehearsal.

Eddie entered and approached Rita: "How's the gate?"

Rita looked at him sternly. "What business is it of yours?"

"Oh, I have a little piece of this place."

"You do, now?"

"I have my fingers in several pies. So how's the gate?"

"A sell out. Pretty good for the first night for a new talent."

"Yeah, well, the word got around."

The lights go down. Once again, the band performs "Enough Is Enough." As a medley, we also hear "One Night Only."

Opening night, the audience was wonderfully warm, but I had sung the songs that I had sung the first night I had become DeeDee. These were expected winners. But now it was time to give them something new. “Ladies and gentlemen, you’ve been such a great audience; you’ve made me feel so welcome and so wonderful. I hope you come back real soon. You know why? Because:

Loving you

Is easy because you're beautiful.”

And when I hit the high notes in the song, the audience was amazed. Out of the corner of my eye, I caught Eddie’s face.

He was completely mesmerized by the performance. Sensual and sweet? Even Rita didn’t expect that. And I noticed a man in a far cheaper suit watching Eddie watching me.

In a private office in an Atlanta precinct, Chief Detective Willie Collins studied a series of photographs on the reverse side of a large bulletin board. There are years of photographs of Eddie. Collins adds one taken moments earlier at the club Hetero. A young lieutenant brings in a series of files and places them on the desk. "'Teflon' Eddie again?"

"Eddie Kingston, in person."

The lieutenant studied the photos more closely. "Hey, how long do these photos go back?"

"High school."

"Damn! You been studying him for that long?"

We went to high school together. He hasn't changed much."

"What do you mean?"

"He was always ultra-charismatic. Could talk anybody into doing anything."

"I guess. Never a gang member but always around some form of organized crime. How come he's never been caught?"

"Because he always get others to do things for him. They love him, so they're loyal, even if they have to go to jail."

Seems like he would have pissed the wrong person off by now."

"Seems like."

13

“Discovery One”

After the last encore, I accepted a large bouquet of flowers. I left the stage and saw Rita talking with Eddie.

“Eddie, you stayed through both sets. How sweet!”

Eddie grinned: "I had to hear you sing 'Loving You' one more time to be sure I could believe my ears. Damn, girl! When you hit those high notes - "

I winked at Rita. "You should hear me go for low notes."

Rita smiled knowingly and nudged me. "Quit bragging, girl."

Eddie looked at Rita and asked, "Can DeeDee and I have a moment alone?"

Rita giggled, and then the giggle became a laugh. "Sho nuff, Player. Knock yo'self out." And Rita withdrew.

Eddie flashed his megawatt smile again. "Congratulations! This is an unqualified triumph!" I smiled demurely. "Why, thank you, sir."

He took and kissed my hand. “Would you like to go out for a late supper?”

I took my hand back. “I don’t think so.”

“Come on, you gotta eat.”

“When you say late supper, do you mean like a date?”

“Well, uh, yeah.”

“No.”

“Okay, DeeDee, you may not like me, but “

“I didn’t say I didn’t like you.”

“Well, then - “

“I’ll go eat with you, but only as friends, not a date.”

Eddie was flummoxed. Women

NEVER turned him down. What should he have said? "All right. We'll go out to supper on your terms. You want to pay, too?"

I looked down my nose at him. "I can afford it."

We both laughed.

For the next few weeks, Eddie and I went out on a whirlwind of expensive "dates" that weren't really dates. The marquees at the Heterosex flashed by: "DeeDee - Third Big Week, Fourth Big Week, Fifth Big Week." Eddie tried his best to seduce me. What was he thinking? Nothing he tried worked on me.

New Year's Eve, I performed a grueling three shows! I tried to keep my energy up; but I am sure I disappointed some of the patrons because I was showing signs of exhaustion at the end of the third show. Several of the staff offered me "various stimulants" but I had vowed never to go down that road and I wasn't going to start.

Rita showed up in the company of a beautiful woman. She introduced her new friend to Eddie, probably to see how he would react since she was so amused by his infatuation with me. "Eddie, this is Monica."

"How do you do, Monica?"

Monica whispered to Rita, "Who is this, Rita? Are you bi?"

"No, not a bit," she answered so that

Eddie could hear her. "But Eddie was talented with his tongue, and I wanted to know what it would be like to be straight, so I found out."

Eddie rolled his eyes.

Rita continued: "So we stayed together because we had such great fights. And now, we have this love-hate relationship."

Trying to change the subject, Eddie asked: "What do you want, Rita?"

"Well, Monica here is a lesbian, but she's white, see, and she's never gone to bed with a black girl, and so she wants to go to bed with me to ring in the new year."

"And?"

"And I'm out of here. If you'll give

DeeDee a ride home, that is."

"Oh, uh, why yes, of course. I'd be delighted."

"And she's dead tired tonight. So just take her home and leave her there. And don't start no shit."

"Who me?"

The party was still very much ringing in the new year as Eddie put me in his Mercedes, a black car with very darkened windows. Eddie hurried energetically over to the driver's side and hopped in. And I took off my shoes. "I hope you don't mind if I slip my shoes off. I swear, I was never meant for women's footwear." Eddie started the car. "As I hear it, nobody was." I could feel myself falling in to a sleep-like stupor. “Oh, Eddie, I’m so sleepy. I forget how I got through half the third set.”

“Well, New Year’s comes but once a year.”

“Thank God,“ I groaned emitting a big yawn.

And I must have fallen asleep then because the next thing I knew, Eddie had stopped the car, parking it. He tried to kiss me but this woke me up like a splash of cold water, and I nudged him away. More determined, Eddie then tried to unbutton my collar and reach my “breasts,” but I turned away from him, guarding my chest, and that left my legs open and unguarded. Eddie put his hand on my knee and slid it up inside my skirt before I could respond.

Eddie screamed: "What the fuck is this? Are you a fag?" I got out of the car. Eddie took his gun out of the glove box. He got out and started shooting above my head and around me. The bullets hit surrounding cars. I was petrified and ducked into Rita's building. Eddie tried to drive his car and find me in the parking lot but lost me in the darkness.

I made my way in horror to Rita's apartment. I had pissed myself.

When Rita entered, I was cowering on the couch, hugging a pillow tightly. Rita didn't notice Donald's state right at first, too excited to tell me about her own adventure. "Oh, baby, you should have seen Monica's place. She has a penthouse in the Ritz

Carlton over up in Buckhead. She had a bathtub that - “ Rita then saw that I was almost in shock. “ - Donald, what the hell is the matter with you?”

“Eddie tried to - He put his hand on me. He put his hand on my knee and ran it up my skirt. He - “ I had expected nurture, sympathy maybe, but my own words were drowned out by Rita’s screaming fits of laughter. “Rita, Eddie knows!”

“Don’t worry about Eddie,” said Rita, still shaking from laughter. “Eddie is such a homophobe that he would never tell anyone for fear that the word would get out. He’d be humiliated, the laughing stock of Atlanta.”

“In that case, he’ll kill me - “

"No, he won't. He won't because he likes you. He won't because he has too much to lose. And he won't because he knows if he did he'd have to deal with me." And with that, Rita pulled out an ice pick.

"Rita. An ice pick?"

"I used to cut myself when I carried a straight razor. But I always have my ice pick with me when we go to the club."

"I'm not going back to the club."

"What do you mean, girl. I signed a contract on behalf of DeeDee - "

"Do you hear me? Eddie was shooting at me; he tried to run me down with his car. I'm not going back."

"Listen, you ARE going back."

"Rita, this is not fun anymore - "

"You ARE going back. I'll protect you."

"My secret is out."

Rita fingered her ice pick. "Your secret is safe. I got this."

Unbeknownst to me, something was going on this New Year's Day in the downtown Atlanta police precinct. Chief Detective was not sleeping in, or watching parades, or preparing snacks for a day of college football. Collins was studying the telefaxes he had received overnight. He asked his lieutenant: "What did we do to draw a shift this early on New Year's Day?"

"I don't know, but I brought a TV. I don't care much for the parades. But some of the bowl games start early."

"What have we here?"

"What? Something interesting?"

"Early this morning, somebody with a forty-five shot up a parking lot downtown."

"So? Niggers is always shooting one another in downtown Atlanta."

Collins looked up disapprovingly, but he decided not to make a big deal out of his lieutenant's profiling. "Oh, no. Nobody got shot this time. Just cars. But the apartment complex had installed one of those cameras that take pictures in the dark. And guess what we got? A picture of a license plate."

The lieutenant poured himself a cup of coffee. "Anybody we know?"

Collins smiled. "Oh, yeah. That license plate is registered to a Mr. Eddie

Rochester Kingston."

"That's our Eddie. Mr. Teflon himself."

"Oh, yeah. Thank you, Jesus."

Looking more carefully at one of the photos, the lieutenant saw a smeared face of - you guessed it DeeDee.

"So who is this?"

14

"I Only Want to Talk."

I couldn't go back to the Heterosex, but Rita did. Business is business, she said, and she was holding out for me to change my mind and return. Rita was going over some of the paperwork and arranging her usual payment to me when Eddie entered wearing a sweat suit. “Rita, I been looking for you.”

Rita didn’t want to be distracted from her business and had no time for Eddie, but she said, “What do you want?” because she wanted to needle him about me. Sometimes I wonder if she were always planning for this confrontation.

“I want to see DeeDee.”

“Why, to hurt her?”

“No, just to talk to her.”

“’Her?’ But you know - ”

“Yeah,

I know. Who else knows?”

“Just me, and DeeDee, and now, you.”

"Are you sure?"

"I'm sure. Nobody else knows."

"I know she's not going home to any mama, and you know where she is, and I want to talk to her."

With a twinkle in her eye, Rita asked, "Are you in love?"

"Don't be a damn fool. I just want to talk to the girl."

Rita waited for a moment, then said: "I'll set it up, but you'd better not fuck with her, or I'll put my ice pick right dead in your eye."

"I only want to talk."

"Be at my place at 6:30."

When I found out about the meeting, I was furious. "6:30! I don't want to see him at all. He’s going to do something -”

Rita shook her head. “No, he won’t. I’ll be here. But you have to do this. And we have just enough time to get you into DeeDee mode.”

“What difference does it make, Rita. He knows I’m a man.”

“Yes, but he only knows you as DeeDee. And we need him to talk with you as DeeDee.”

And so Rita set about transforming me into DeeDee again. Not for a club performance, but for a real life performance, which is what I intended the masquerade to be in the first place before it got out of hand. at 6:30, Rita let Eddie in. I was sitting on the couch. Rita looked at me, then turned back to Eddie. “I’ll be in my bedroom. You remember what I said?”

Eddie nodded. “If I want to keep this eye - “

But Rita didn’t wait for him to finish. She withdrew. It took Eddie a long time to decide what to say to me. And when he did, all that came out was, “Hello.”

And equally inane, after a long pause, I also said, “Hello.” Eddie fidgeted for a few moments so I asked him, “Would you like a drink?”

“Yeah. Yeah. A drink would be nice.”

I rose from the couch, went to the kitchen, poured Eddie the Turkey and soda that I knew that he liked, and gave it to him. We sat quietly at the kitchen table.

"I wanted to apologize for acting the fool. I was wrong to become so - but damn! You understand why -

"You had no damn business putting your hand between my legs. So don't put this on me. You know I never wanted a physical relationship, or a romance at all. Just friends -

"Okay. Okay. Okay. I didn't come here to argue with you." Eddie took a long pull on his drink. "I accept full blame for - "

"Then why are you here?"

"Because I miss you."

"It hasn't been that long - "

"I mean that if you stay away I will miss you."

"What? Miss me performing with the

band?"

"Of course, that. And I miss your - " Eddie struggled with his words. " - presence. I want to be around you - "

"But you know who I am. You know what I am."

"Yes. That's true. I don't really understand, but I miss you. Will you come back?"

I tilted my head back and took a deep breath. "I did sign a contract. If I don't come back, I'll be in hot water
with 'management.' So I must come back to work -

Surprising me, Eddie grabbed my hand. "I think I have - " He stopped. I looked at his face; he looked confused.

"I have feelings for you."

For some strange reason, I almost laughed. "You're not - "

Eddie was irritated. "Hell, no, I'm not. You know I'm not."

I was trying my best to understand. "Then what is this all about?"

Eddie shook his head. "I can't explain it."

And then we didn't say anything else. We simply looked at one another for a long time

15

"Good Company"

I had always suspected that Sly and Fox, a couple of guys who always seemed within a short distance of Eddie, were meandering through the crowd at the Heterosex Club. I saw money changing hands and packets of some powder being placed in pockets. Business was good for them. All because Artie and I had put together a new show. Midway through the first set, the audience was as usual, loving every minute of it. I tried to quiet the audience down with limited effect.

"Everybody feelin' all right? Now, how many of you Atlanta faithful remember the Georgia Satellites?"

The audience yelled and applause was everywhere whether they remembered the group or not. A beat began behind me, something between funk and country - for our audience, the best of both worlds.

"Well, we wanted to cover one of their best songs tonight. Have a little fun?

So we asked Rick Richards, formerly their lead guitar player, to join us for a little old Atlanta jam. All right?"

With the audience's assent, I added: "Here we go! This one's for Eddie."

Eddie was surprised, but he also seemed to be intrigued. So I launched into the song, the one about "no huggin', no kissin', without a wedding ring." And each time I sang "Don't give me no lines and keep your hands to yourself," the audience would roar and Eddie would seethe. Did he think this was my revenge? Did he think I was ridiculing him? But, oddly enough, on the third time through, Eddie started to laugh. He led the applause as I writhed back to back with Rick Richards. I was back, baby!

I was back!

The next day, Eddie took me to the park. He pushed me in a swing. Both of us glowed with joy, friends again.

"Your new show is a major success," said Eddie, keenly grasping the obvious. "Did you enjoy your song?"

"Ouch! Yes, during the first two verses, I was grinding my teeth, but when I saw what a good time you were having, I realized that you were just playing."

"I had to come up with a way to keep you from taking everything so seriously."

"You got me. You got me."

"Eddie, have you ever had a relationship that wasn't sexual?" I stopped swinging.

Eddie had stopped pushing me and sat on the other swing. He thought about my question and explained: "There was this girl I dated in high school and I idolized her. Would you believe I saved myself for anybody? Then, she got pregnant. My goddess got knocked up - " I could hear the hurt in his voice. " - by somebody else. So I figured, why put anybody else on a pedestal? I NEVER get turned down. Not 'til you."

"What happened to the girl?"

Eddie shrugged. "Botched abortion. Dead and gone. Her brother was, is a cop. Blamed me. Never would listen to my side."

"Here's the thing, Eddie. How much of any relationship is sex? How much of the fun is actually doing something else? Since neither one of us is gay, yet we both seem to be unhappy without keeping company with one another, why not agree to do everything couples who love each other do - other than the kissing and the sex?

"You mean - "

"We hug. We tell each other that we love each other. You know, guy stuff, except only we know that I'm a guy. We go shopping, and on dates, and everything couples do

except the kissing and the sex."

And then, Eddie began to laugh. He laughed harder than I had ever heard him laugh. "The idea is insane," Eddie said, "yet it makes complete sense."

And so we agreed on the terms of our relationship. To celebrate, Eddie bought himself a classic Jaguar XK-E.

And as Eddie bought his Jaguar , Detective Collins studied the latest photographs. The lieutenant came in with coffee for both, saying: “I thought that shoot-em-up would
put Eddie in our hands for sure.”

“I thought so, too. But Eddie’s got a crack attorney and a license for that gun.”

“Shit.”

“These pictures may help us, Lieutenant, still.” He showed the lieutenant a night photo and a very recent photo.
“I think we’ve identified the stimulus for the shooting incident.” That stimulus was me.

I was touching up my DeeDee makeup. Rita appeared. I smiled at her. “Good crowd tonight, huh?”

Rita nodded: “You got ‘em in the palm of your hand, baby girl. You want to do something after the show?”

“No. Eddie’s picking me up - “

“You never drive that car he bought you?”

“That he bought me? Is that what he told you?” I shook my head. “It’s in the shop again. Cars like that are sensitive. They have to be pampered. Maybe he’ll give it to me when it’s running properly.

“Uh-huh. Sounds like Eddie bought you a lemon.”

“No! When a Jag is running right, it

purrs like a kitten."

Rita shook her head.

Eddie was not around that night; he was shooting craps. He'd been losing big time. A large man moved to Eddie's side. He whispered, "You told me to tell you when it's two a.m."

Eddie nodded. "I'm too far in the hole." He thought for a moment, then added: "Rita will give her a ride." Eddie then put several hundreds on a hard eight.

The show was over and I was looking for Eddie. Sly and Fox pulled up. They were driving a classic Versailles in perfect condition. I could hear Sly say, "Hey, it's DeeDee!"

And Fox added, "Hey, girl! Can we

get your autograph?"

"That's sweet, fellows, but I'm waiting on my -boyfriend."

Sly and Fox exchanged glances. "You mean Eddie?" Sly asked.

Fox added, "We know Eddie." He got out and opened the back door of the car and gestured grandly. "Sit in the back seat. We'll keep you good company while you wait."

"No, thanks. I'll - "

"Please," begged Sly. "It's almost never that we get to talk with a real star."

"I wouldn't call myself that."

"Yeah, but

we would," said Fox. "Girl, you the toast of Atlanta."

Sly sang, "And baby, it's cold outside."

"And don't worry about us," Fox smiled. "We're friends of Eddie's and we know you're a real lady."

This amused me and it was cold so I got into the car.

Eddie was still losing badly when the large man interrupted him again. "Rita on the phone, boss."

Eddie rolled his eyes. He tapped out and then spoke angrily to the pit boss. "This table's cold." He got no response. He walked over to the big man who handed him the phone. "What the hell do you want? Did you take DeeDee home?"

"That's your job, stud. Didn't you get

her? I thought you - "

"Shit."

Eddie's powerful Mercedes streaked up Peachtree Street to the Heterosex. He screeched to a halt. He hopped out looking for me but I was distracted. He entered the club; I saw him when he came back out. When I got out of the Versailles, I was still laughing from my conversation with my "two fans."

"What the fuck is going on?" asked Eddie, enraged.

"Calm down, baby," I soothed. "I'm not mad. Sly and Fox have been telling me stories about - " And the Versailles pulled away. I assumed Sly and Fox knew the kind of mood Eddie was in and decided to leave to let Eddie cool down.

"You think you're a real bitch, or something? Getting in the back seat - "

"Eddie, nothing happened!"

I got into Eddie's car which was a mistake. Eddie hadn't calmed down. He peeled off down the street driving like a maniac, heading toward Stone Mountain. I looked at the dials and saw that Eddie's speedometer registered over a hundred. It was amazing that no police were out to make chase.

"You think you're a real bitch now, huh?"

"Eddie, you shouldn't be talking to me like that."

"Bitch, I'll talk to you any way I

like."

"If you're going to talk to me like that, you can just let me out of the car right here." This was also bad judgment since we were already out in a rural area and I could see no homes or cars around.

"Oh, is that so?" Eddie slammed on his brakes. The car spun around. but Eddie kept control until it ground to a halt. "You get your wish."

I gave Eddie a long hurt stare. "Eddie, why can't you believe me? Nothing happened. Sly and Fox were nice to me. They didn't try - "

"Get the fuck out of my car, bitch!"

I didn't move. Like a machine, Eddie got out, went to the other side, opened the door, roughly pulled me out of the car, slammed the door, got back in, and with a screech of tires, drove away. I watched until his car was out of sight. He was not coming back for me.

I walked back toward Atlanta. I realized that my high heels were not making the trip any easier, so I took my shoes off and resumed my trek.

16

“A Lady Shouldn’t Be Walking”

Eddie went back to the crap game. He was steaming angry. And his success with the dice was no better.

I was walking back to Atlanta. My

feet were bleeding a little bit and I had stopped to examine them when three men in a pickup truck pulled up beside me and looked closely, amazed to find such a "hot girl" on the open road early in the morning. The fellow on my side of the truck rolled down a window.

"Hey? What you doing all the way out here?"

"Walking back to Atlanta."

"Walking? A lady like you shouldn't be walking. It's not safe."

"I'll manage."

The driver shouted, "No southern gentleman would let a
lady walk that far."

I looked at the three passengers.

"Looks like you have a full load."

The truck pulled to a stop.

The man closest to me said: "It really seats four, but I'll get in the back to make more room."

I replied, "No, thank you."

But the man got out of the truck and said, "Really, I don't mind. I like a cool morning breeze."

"In February?"

"Missy, this is Hotlanta."

The second man got out, too and held the door open for me. I knew better than to get in but my eyes caught the sign that said "Atlanta 20 miles." I looked at my sore and nicked feet. These guys didn't seem threatening, so against my better judgment, I got in the truck. The man holding the door got in beside me, and the driver smiled. The man on the outside jumped into the back of the truck and the truck got back on the highway. But the truck didn't stay on the highway long. Instead, they turned off on a dirt road through the woods behind a thicket off the interstate. The truck bounced down the road. I tried to get out of the truck, but the men prevented me although I was obviously stronger than they had expected.

We arrived at a clearing not far into the woods. The truck stopped and the men threw me into the back. They tried their best to both restrain me and also take off my clothes, but I put up a good fight. When they started to get the best of me, I decided to beg. “Please, don’t do this. You don’t want to do this.” But they continued until I was undressed.

“God damn!” screamed the driver. “This here’s a man.”

Their thoughts now turning away from rape, they pulled me from the back and kicked and beat me. They took bottles and used them as clubs until they broke. Finally, in the ultimate indignity, one of the men urinated on me. The driver got back into the truck and circled, picking up the other two. As they headed for the highway, I tried to lift myself and was grazed by the bumper of the truck. I didn’t realize how close to death I had come. I simply had to try to read the license plate, “477 - “ But the truck disappeared. I rose and found enough pieces of my clothing to put together a loin cloth.

I limped up the road to the interstate where I stumbled. A car saw poor crumpled me and pulled over to help.

I was placed in an ambulance by a couple of paramedics.

One got inside with me, the other drove. With light and siren on, the ambulance headed for Emory Hospital in Atlanta. By that time, I was drifting into a fog. And I didn't like it. You know how I want to remain in control at all times.

I had various cuts and head wounds so the intensive care staff was forced to shave my head. I tried my best to protest but realized that my lack of movement and my inability to find my voice must have meant that I was in a coma. A male nurse was in charge while a female nurse bathed me. I heard her speak as she lifted my arm. “Hey, Charlie . When did guys start shaving their pits?”

“Well, some athletes do. But mostly, that custom is left to trannies.”

“Oh, my God. I know who John Doe, here, is.”

“Yeah?”

“This is DeeDee, the singer down at the Heterodrome or whatever that place is called. I heard she was about to cut an album.”

“She?”

"That's what I thought until now. Damn! Everybody thinks DeeDee is female. This could be big news."

Rita was puttering around and turned on the TV. The noon news showed a photo of "DeeDee" at the club. ". . . In the Emory Hospital today as celebrity DeeDee lies in a coma after what appears to have been a severe beating. DeeDee has been revealed to be a male entertainer, even though his soprano performances have been hailed as the purest since the death of the late Minnie Riperton. More information is being withheld until next of
kin . . ."

Rita rushed to dress.

Once she arrived, Rita was told that

she could not go in to see me. She protested: “I’m her manager.”

“If you’ll calm down,” the nurse was reconsidering.

Rita was still in a state but steeled herself and nodded.

“She’s still in a very fragile state,” the nurse cautioned, oddly referring to me as feminine. “If you speak to DeeDee, calmly? Well, sometimes that helps.” And she added, “I’m a fan.”

Rita nodded and approached the bed and from her facial expression, I must have looked worse than she had expected.

“Oh, baby. What did he do to you? Eddie did this to you, didn’t he?”

I squinted, hoping Rita would see and

interpret. She saw my squint but took this as a yes and left, determined to find Eddie. She was not aware that she was being watched as she left. When he was sure that Rita was gone, Chief Detective Collins stepped out from behind a screen and came over to me. I am certain that I still looked distressed. He took my hand: "DeeDee, I'm Willie Collins, chief detective, Atlanta police. Can you hear me? If you can hear me, squeeze my hand. If you can hear me, squeeze my hand."

Very lightly, I increased my grip on Collins' hand.

"You know, Eddie has a history of treating women badly." What he had said to me was absurd; surely, he knew that I am a man. He sat on what little edge there was on the narrow bed and spoke gently. “Did Eddie do this to you, DeeDee? Squeeze my hand if he hurt you.”

Nothing.

“Was it because he discovered that you are - I can see that he never hurts anyone like this again. Squeeze my hand if Eddie did this.

Still nothing. Collins placed my hand back on the bed, gently, rose, and stepped outside the alcove. He turned to the nurse who was a fan.

“Get any clues from DeeDee?”

“I know who did this. I just can’t get her to confirm it.”

“Her? The illusion. You fell into the trap.”

Both were amused. She and Collins exchanged a long smile before he left. I thought to myself, "Who am I, anyway?" And then, I drifted into a dreamless sleep.

Rita had tracked Eddie to the "boutique casino" and knocked on the door - three, then two, then four. The large man looked out the door.

"I need to speak to Eddie."

"He's not here."

"I know he's here; get him out here."

"He don't want to see nobody. He's winnin' again."

"Tell him it's an emergency and to get his ass out here now."

After a pause, the large man closed the door. Rita waited. Eddie returned and stepped outside, saying: "Now what the fuck do you want?"

"Why'd you do DeeDee that way?"

"She deserved it. I caught her in a car, acting the bitch with two shifty niggers."

"Well, you didn't have to beat her!" And with that, Rita went for Eddie's eye with the ice pick. Eddie successfully blocked the blow with his arm, but the ice pick punctured his upper arm. Painfully, Eddie wrenched Rita into a wrestling hold, his wounded arm around her neck.

"What do you mean, beat her? I didn't beat her."

"Liar. You put her in the hospital, beat her so bad, she's in a coma."

"She told me to put her out of the car.

I put her out of the car and drove away."

"I don't believe you," said Rita. But Rita was no fool, and she knew that Eddie would own up to it had he done the deed. "Where?"

"I don't know. Stone Mountain, I think."

"Stone Mountain? You crazy bastard! You left her by herself out by Stone Mountain?"

"She told me to. Now, what hospital is she in."

"Emory."

Eddie hurried toward Emory Hospital. He winced from the pain in his arm, but the puncture wound showed nothing other than a small dot of red.

Eddie stormed past the nurses and came into my alcove.

I sensed his presence and realized that he was sobbing. Still, I could not say anything. Nurse Nancy went to her station phone and called Collins. Chief Detective Collins? You asked me to call you if any person of interest entered DeeDee's alcove?"

Eddie's wound started to bleed and trickle down his hand, dripping on the floor. The nurse saw the blood on the floor, so she approached Eddie. "Sir, we need to look at that arm."

Eddie pushed her away, harder than he intended to, I'm sure, leaving the nurse sprawling. "Get away from me." He walked over to me and whispered. “Baby, I’m gonna find out who did this to you and then I’m gonna kill ‘em.” He tenderly kissed me on the only uninjured square inch of skin on my face. Then, he stormed out of the room.

Nurse Charlie came in to help Nurse Nancy up. “I’m all right.”

And they both heard me cry out feebly: “Eddie?”

17

“The Face on the Billboard”

I was awake. I was sitting up, sort of, and talking.

Collins came in again. He looked at the room, at the floor. Eddie’s blood had not been mopped away. Nurse Nancy pointed at the blood.

"I didn't want to mop that up, thought it might be a clue." She and Collins shared another look.

"Was Eddie here?" I asked

Collins stepped to the bedside. "Yes, DeeDee. Eddie was here. Just say the word and I'll have him behind bars without bail. You don't have to protect him - "

"Eddie didn't do this to me. Eddie couldn't do this to me. Eddie and I are friends."

Collins looked confused. "But Eddie has a history of abusing women. He got his high school girl friend pregnant and left her to - "

"No, he didn't. Eddie put on the mask of a player, but he chose to stay a virgin out of honoring that girl. It nearly killed him to find out she was pregnant. What was
that girl's name? Do you know? Eddie said her brother became a cop."

Things were fuzzy.

Distracted, Collins asked me hesitantly, "Do you remember anything about who did this to you?"

"Three guys in a pickup truck. License plate started off 477 something. I think it was grey; it was dark, though. Wish I could tell you more."

Collins smiled faintly. "That should help. Excuse me, but back New Year's, didn't

Eddie shoot at you?"

"Eddie didn't shoot at me. He was just shooting because he was mad that he couldn't screw me."

I managed to smile, too. Collins and the two nurses exchanged glances as if to say: "What the hell?"

Eddie was sitting in his car, in an alley somewhere, in downtown Atlanta. The police lieutenant who usually shadowed Detective Collins handed Eddie some paperwork. He said: "So DeeDee knew part of the plate. A blue/gray pickup truck belonging to a Wilson Reeves over there from Forsythe; Georgia plate number 477 - GMV. Runs a small construction

company. Anyway, those guys hang out in a

club in east Atlanta. Well, not really a club. More just a beer joint. The name is the Dew Drop Inn. Here's the address." The lieutenant handed the stack of papers to Eddie; Eddie
handed the lieutenant a lot of money.

Later, across the street from the Dew Drop Inn, Eddie watched from his car. He saw the pickup truck pull up and park. He looked at his 45 and a matching pistol. He wore a black jump suit. He stepped out of the car to head across the street, but as soon as he did, an unmarked police car and a squad car pulled in across the street. Two policemen and Chief Detective Collins charged into the street, armed and wearing flak jackets. Eddie got back in his car and watched them.

Three guys from the truck and the three policemen came back out. The guys from the truck were hand-cuffed and their legs were chained together. As Eddie watched, a couple of other men walked up to the Inn and saw the police and turned and ran. Collins ordered the other cops to pursue them. When they turned the corner, Collins prepared to put the trio in the back of his car. So Eddie made his move. He went charging across the street, guns in both hands. Collins pulled his gun and shouted: "No! Eddie! No!" But Collins did not shoot.

The three guys from the truck were like fish in a barrel because they were chained together. Eddie unloaded about four slugs in each and kept coming.

Collins yelled: “Eddie, don’t make me shoot you!” He and Eddie made eye contact. Eddie nodded at Collins and pointed one of his pistols in Collins’ direction.

The other officers returned with their two suspects. They did not hesitate; they shot Eddie three times fast. Eddie fell to the street. Collins charged out to where Eddie had fallen and took Eddie’s head in his lap. Blood dribbled from the edge of Eddie’s mouth.

“Eddie. Why’d you do this? Why?”

“Had to get those guys. And my rep was ruined so - tell your boys over there that they did me a favor.” Eddie coughed up blood. "You tell DeeDee that I got those guys."

"I will. I will."

"You tell DeeDee that I love her. You tell her."

If Collins found the dichotomy of all this appalling, he didn't say so. "Yes, Eddie. I will."

And Eddie was dead.

But Collins hugged him and rocked him and kept talking: "I never hated you, Eddie. I wanted to be like you. I admired you. You were like a brother that I never had. But then you were dogging my sister. Oh, why didn't you tell me that - ?" And the rest was sobbing.

My parents pulled their station wagon

up to the hospital. Rita pushed the wheel chair out. My dad helped me into the back seat.

Mom looked back at Rita as Rita handed baskets of flowers to Dad to situate in the back around the wheel chair. “I’m Donald’s mother. Are you Donald’s girl friend?

Rita smiled painfully. “Yes, ma’am, something like that.”

“Well, then, you’ll have to come see us up in Chattanooga when Donald gets to feeling better.”

Rita smiled and nodded. “I’d like that.”

I motioned for Rita to hug me and whispered: “You know, I loved Eddie.”

"I know. He loved you, too. In his way, he gave his life for you."

"How much of all this do my parents know?"

"They just got here. They don't know anything."

I thought about this. I had no idea what I was going to tell them. But they were back in earshot, so I let her go.

"Thank you for everything," Mom said. Rita stood and received a hug from Betty.

Then, Bill offered his hand and received a firm handshake from Rita. "Thank you for taking care of my son.

Rita smiled and nodded: "My pleasure."

Dad turned the corner by the hospital.

He drove down to the red light at the next corner. On an electrical pole was a glossy cardboard poster for the Hetero with a great picture of DeeDee singing.

"Donald, did you get to see this DeeDee while you were here?"

"Not exactly."

"Bill, I heard this girl is fabulous. She can sing and dance. She puts on a wonderful show. Baby, if she ever comes to Chattanooga, would you please take me?"

"Okay, Betty. If she ever comes, I'll take you to see her. Meanwhile, how about a little Billie Holliday?

"Always welcome," crooned Mom.

Dad put a cassette tape in as the light changes. It started to rain. Billie sang “My Man” and the station wagon merged into traffic. High above on a billboard that my parents didn’t see was a huge duplicate of the poster. Reading “Held Over! Again! DeeDee with Artie Black’s Band. Live at the Hetero! For reservations call . . .”

As we listened to Billie sing and as the station wagon headed home to Chattanooga, I cried and said a little silent prayer for Eddie.